MOONBOW

PREQUEL TO THE PETROS CHRONICLES

DIANA ANDERSON-TYLER

Published by Diana Tyler 2015

Copyright © 2015 Diana Tyler

www.dianaandersontyler.com

Book cover design and formatting services by BookCoverCafe.com

First Edition 2015

ISBN: 978-0-692-47472-3

TABLE OF CONTENTS

This book is dedicated to the two greatest men in my life: my ever-loving, ever-patient, ever-encouraging, ever-kind husband Ben who persistently requested that I write more pages for him to read, and to my ever-wise, ever-imaginative, ever-fascinating, ever-heroic, ever-inspiring father Mitchell who, even in Heaven, whispers to me, "pray always, and no matter what, keep smiling."

PROLOGUE

I grew up in a family that embraced religion; they respected and revered it above anything else. My mother and father were devout followers of Duna, the preeminent and only Eusebian god, and taught my brother Jasper and me about the prophecies, prophecies that had been handed down to our people for thousands of years. Prophecies that promised us freedom from the Alphas, and peace that would be unbreakable. My parents yearned for the day when the Promised One would appear and defeat Python, signaling a new beginning.

My father had been at the Temple the day Phos was dedicated as a baby, long before Jasper or I was ever born. He told my mother he'd seen Duna's son. He knew without question that this baby would grow up to be the savior of us all.

My father never lived to find out that Phos died a martyr, not a savior. A criminal, not a king.

My mother was on her death bed when Jasper brought her the news that Phos had been killed in the Great Sea, and using every bit of strength she had left, she whispered, "It's as Duna said it would be. It isn't over...it isn't over..."

Like my mother's body, my faith died slowly. It weakened little by little after she died, until one day, our most sacred holy day, I refused to go to the temple. Why worship a god who had taken my parents from me and allowed his followers to be subjugated by a people that treated us like swine? Our god must despise us, not love us. But what had we done to offend him? And though I loved my brother, I never pretended to pay any attention to his sermons and prayers when he too became a believer in Phos. His faith was his way of coping. Without it, he had no hope.

There's only been one thing that has given me hope – the legend of the doma.

The doma is a gift – or some might say a power – that was given to my family ages ago, when the Moonbow first appeared. My ancestor, Asher, was one of the first Eusebian Oracles, and one of the last to whom Duna spoke directly. At least, that's what we're brought up to believe.

The legend goes that Asher was woken one night by a cold wind and a thunderous voice from heaven. That voice, the voice of Duna, called him up to the headlands above the Great Sea. Endless bolts of lightning ripped through the sky, and the rain was so sharp and the wind so fierce that Asher feared for his life. He ducked into a grove of olive trees and waited. After a few minutes, he listened as the wind faded to a whisper and the rain softened to a gentle shower. He carefully stepped out beneath the open sky and saw the full moon hanging valiantly and the storm clouds dissolving to nothingness in the stars.

"Asher..." called the voice. Then he turned from the moon and watched in awe as the fingertips of Duna began to paint the arches of the first Moonbow, one by one, onto the smoky black palette of sky.

Duna instructed Asher to write down what was happening, but Asher lamented:

"But, my King! I have not a stylus, nor a tablet to do what you say!"

Asher's heart was heavy with longing. He so desperately desired to describe what he saw that he tore his garments and he sunk both hands into the soft wet earth. Feeling something materializing in his right hand, he pulled it out and was astonished to see a stylus wedged between his fingers. By the light of the Moonbow, he marveled as a mound of mud beside him transformed itself into a coarse loaf of tablet clay.

It was the first doma. And with it, he recorded the prophecy of the Moonbow, that it would no longer be seen again until his son, Phos, had defeated Python in the Great Sea, winning victory and freedom for all of us. Duna told him that from that day forward, the line of Asher would carry the colors of the Moonbow in their gifts.

For Asher, the tablet he pulled from the earth turned from ochre to bright red, symbolizing the first arch of the Moonbow. Asher could make tablets from any part of nature he wished, be it grass, or sand, snow, or salt. And with them, he obediently recorded what Duna told him to for the rest of his days. Much of what he wrote are the prophecies and parables that have been repeated to me since the day I was born.

Not everyone in my family is an Asher, as those with a doma are called. Duna revealed that only one child per household would manifest a power the year they became an adult, which in Eusebian culture, is age eighteen.

My grandmother's gift represented the fifth arch of the Moonbow. With it, she could produce enough water to fill seven pots using only a single drop of liquid. Her doma supplied enough water for her family and neighbors during the drought, back when my mother was still a baby. None of her children, not my mother, nor her two younger brothers, received a doma. It was believed that the gift belonged to their baby sister, my aunt Corinna, who disappeared while she was still a girl. Most believe she was kidnapped by a Pythonian, but no one ever knew for sure. Eusebians are commanded by the Oracles to keep the Ashers' identities concealed from the Alphas lest someone try to take advantage of the doma, or destroy it, but I'm sure there have been mistakes...perhaps accidental, perhaps blatant.

Jasper didn't receive a doma, and he was twenty-one when he died. I turned eighteen eleven months ago, and still I am waiting to see if Duna has remembered me and kept his promise. If he has, maybe then I can avenge my brother by killing my master...his murderer. And after that, maybe I can have my life back. Time will tell. Either way, my master's days are numbered, a fact that motivates me to wake up and serve him each morning, far more than does the fear of encountering his ruthless whip.

CHAPTER ONE
IRIS

The pyres seem peaceful on the water, rocking gently in a cradle of cobalt waves. If I were a foreigner walking far off, I would think fishermen were merely casting their nets on a temperate evening. But I know better. The Sea of Enochos is not a place for catching fish, but for burning men alive.

Strapped to floating piles of wood are my brother and four others, all helpless, yet each one perfectly still in their final moments of life. Those gathered around me on the pebbled shore shiver as the clouds collide and sink slowly like shrouds around the condemned. But I do not shiver, because instead of cold air on my skin, I feel sharp arrows of heat shooting through my veins. Anger and hatred boil deep inside my heart and bubble up as sweat on my brow and lip. All I can do to restrain myself from shouting out in my brother's defense is clench my fists so hard that my nails bite into my skin.

A small vessel appears like a phantom before the pyres. The cloaked executioner upon it stands tall and lifts something into the air with his right hand. He ignites it for us all to see...the torch. Its orange flame, boldly illuminating the place of death with each haunting flicker, sends a chill down my spine. I shiver like the rest.

The executioner wields the hungry torch and strikes the first pyre with a harsh unfeeling grunt. Within seconds, the wooden heap is engulfed in a torrent of flames. The crowd begins to murmur until abruptly silenced by the horrific din of wailing as the next three pyres catch fire.

My brother's is the last. I cannot see his face, only his silhouette etched into a cloudless patch of sapphire sky as the executioner's torch draws near to him.

I kneel down and scoop up a handful of pebbles from the water's edge and cup them tenderly in my hands. My brother and I collected thousands of these stones together as children, never tiring of their smooth round shape and splendid hues. Most of all, we had treasured the ones made of jasper, the blood-red rock for which he was named.

Jasper...

Furiously, I throw the pebbles into the sea and cry out as I return my gaze to the shadowy pyre. The torch reaches out to it, and so do I.

I fling my body into the frigid water and begin swimming toward him, but not with the desire to save him. No, I want to join him, to bind myself beside him and perish with the pebbles beneath me.

The last thing I remember is the feeling of ice in my blood.

⚜

I jump to consciousness, coughing uncontrollably as if ridding my lungs of the bone-chilling salt water that was flooding my nightmare. I snatch the jasper pebble from under my straw mat and hold it tight to my chest.

"Get up!" rasps a voice.

I look up to see Niobe, my master's favorite slave, swaying over me wearing a dead burgundy fox around her shoulders.

"Acheron requests you," she says. The strong smell of wine on her breath wafts toward me.

"It's not morning yet. Can't you see?" I say, pointing to the darkness filling the small window of my chamber. "His needs are yours to see to now."

Niobe's smile fades. Proudly lifting her chin, she spins around unsteadily, revealing the leather cords of Acheron's favorite whip falling from her fists. She turns her head to look at me. "Don't make it worse for yourself, Iris," she whispers. "The punishment will be over quickly if you don't fight it this time."

"Wait!" I shout, pulling my cloak around me as I rise to my feet. "What wrong have I done?" I demand.

Niobe steps forward into the doorway. "You haven't done anything. It's what our people have done. I'm sorry." She leaves me in silence, and I know I have no choice but to follow.

Overcome by a sudden rush of weakness, I lie back onto my mat and close my eyes, savoring just a few moments more of painlessness, and yet pining for the flames of the pyre...

I've been whipped and beaten countless times since Acheron dragged me out of Enochos's grasp three years ago and made me his slave. I swore to myself that I would never forgive him for my brother's death, or from stealing death from me. Perhaps it is shameful, but I am not ashamed to admit that I have imagined taking my own life, with noose and with knife. But I have never attempted suicide. Though my brother and parents are dead, I know that killing myself would break their hearts. Life, my father taught, was a gift. We didn't choose when or how to begin it, so neither should we choose when and how to end it.

Acheron reclines on a wooden couch adorned with bits of gold, tortoise shell, and ivory. He lifts his head from the lilac feather-stuffed pillow supporting it and plucks a slice of pork from a silver stand nearby. Dropping the morsel onto his tongue, he casually waves for me to come closer.

The stone floor beneath me is covered with small pieces of glass, some winter-gray, others emerald-green. It forms a mosaic ribbon which weaves its way from the cypress door to the marble terrace overlooking the River Styx flowing just beyond the open wall.

The Styx, legend tells, is the boundary between this world and Abussos where the spirits of the dead wait to be reborn. It is forbidden to swim or sail the river because the waters, the Alphas say, bring a fatal curse to any mortal trespasser. Jasper told me he slipped and fell into it while hunting a stag along the dew-drenched riverbank one morning and was nearly drowned by a creature he couldn't see.

"I called out to Duna, and then it released me," he swore.

I thought perhaps Jasper's imagination had gotten the better of him, but now, as I gaze at the flawless river I walk upon, I wonder if the Styx truly did seal my brother's fate so long ago...

"You don't want to die a miserable death like your poor brother, do you girl?" Acheron asks, picking a cluster of crimson grapes from a platter Niobe offers him.

Only once in three years has my master spoken my name. He asked for it the morning after he kidnapped me from the execution as Niobe pushed spoonfuls of lentil soup between my lips.

"Iris," I replied.

"Iris," Acheron repeated with a wry smile. "Esteemed goddess of the rainbow! Messenger between us lowly mortals and the omnipotent deities that dictate the trifling affairs of men," he said, bowing with mock adoration. "How marvelous it is to make your acquaintance." He reached down, took my hand, and kissed it softly.

"Niobe, I must commend you. You've done a fine job nursing our honorable guest back to health. Perhaps the gods will crown you Healing Goddess of Hypothermia, should Iris be so gracious as to utter your name on Olympus."

"My family never believed in such fantasies," I said.

"A true Eusebian..." Acheron said, drawing out the words with equal parts curiosity and disdain. "I've always wondered at a people who could so easily scoff at the ancient myths, the gods and their silly stories, and yet worship with unrivaled piety a creator who has left his followers to endure in servitude, completely powerless..."

Niobe placed a cup of wine in my hands and rose to face Acheron. "Duna did not abandon us," she said dauntlessly. "Phos has come and suffered, and the Moonbow appeared, just as the Oracles said it would. We won't be slaves forever."

"Dearest Niobe," Acheron whispered, stroking her cheek. "The moment I think you've discovered some sense you say such stupid things."

He removed his hand from her face and then slapped it hard. "I would like breakfast now, my darling." Niobe bowed her head meekly and rushed out of the room as Acheron turned his attention back to me.

"Tell me. Do you believe the Moonbow to be the promise of freedom as the Eusebians do? Surely you must know, Goddess of the Rainbow..." he said, sardonic laughter betraying his reverence.

Without pausing for an instant to craft a preserving lie, I spoke the truth. "I'd sooner believe that I am as you call me, master."

I present myself to Acheron who has risen to the edge of the couch to retrieve a napkin from the far side of the silver pedestal.

"Eusebian rebels seem to be growing bolder by the day," begins Acheron. "Killing Alpha sentries, stealing their horses, inciting chaos in the streets... It pains me to think of you or dear Niobe behaving so barbarically." He takes my hands in his, looking at me with a pauper's pitiful eyes. "Do you wish to betray me, girl?"

Betray? Am I that obvious, I think. I fight to keep my lips from smiling. In fact, betraying Acheron is my greatest wish, closely following the wish to kill him in cold blood.

My failure to respond aloud replaces the false suffering in Acheron's face with raw, virulent fury. "Niobe, bring me my whip," he commands, wiping his mouth. He stands and impatiently snatches the whip from Niobe's hand. "Have you gone deaf, goddess? Answer my question!"

He begins pacing, madly whipping the mosaic floor with every drunken step. "Do you wish to be tied to a pile of willow branches, set on fire, and have your flesh eaten away, your ashes left for fish food as your brother's were?" He stops just inches from my face, tilts my chin up toward him, and waits for my answer.

I feel Niobe's hands behind me removing my cloak. "No master, I don't want to betray you," I say, careful not to grimace at his foul-smelling breath.

"Good, goddess. I wouldn't want it for you." He spins on his leather boot, then stands motionless, letting silence commence my punishment.

The first lash across my shoulder blades knocks me to my hands and knees.

"You must never speak a word – not even a whisper – of rebellion. No running around stirring up the masses like those heathen rats," Acheron barks, bringing the whip down again, and again, and again...

Face down on the glass river I feel warm streams of blood start to surface on my back. "You shall not be so ignorant. You will know what the punishment is for such stupidity before you sneak away...little... Eusebian... rat!"

Acheron's breathing accelerates and I count seventeen strong strikes until at last his strength gives out. The lashings weaken.

I hear him stumble back onto his couch and take a swig of wine. "I rescued you that night from the madness of the execution. The scars will fade in time...unless your loyalty fails your conscience."

As if sealing the threat, Acheron splashes his wine onto my throbbing wounds. My open flesh drinks it in and I cannot stop my tears.

"Stand, goddess!" Somehow, with head spinning and limbs shaking, I rise as red rivulets trickle down my legs. Acheron holds his right hand in a fist across his chest. "As a proud Guardian of Petros, I salute you!"

Acheron sneers at the drops of blood falling fast onto the floor. "Niobe will clean up the mess. And when the time is right, you will clean up hers."

Coughing pitifully, he sits again, tosses the whip aside, and kicks his feet up onto a pillow. "Now fetch some water. My throat has gone dry." With that, his eyes close and he's swallowed into sleep.

From the watery periphery of my eye, I watch Niobe scurry out of the room. Perhaps she knows it is only a matter of time before the floor beneath her becomes stained with her own Eusebian blood. Perhaps she knows that the Oracles are fools, that her hope is vanity, and that the Moonbow is nothing more than white light entering rain.

CHAPTER TWO
CARYA

The clay water pot feels like a granite boulder in my trembling hands. I stop on the side of the street to rest, and as the world seems to curl up like a shadowy scroll before me, I sit and begin to wonder about the severity of my wounds. I reach under my tunic and gingerly slide my fingers along my side. I shudder to feel the steady flow of warm pulsing life exiting my body, and I know the damage is more severe than Acheron intended.

Squeezing my eyes, willing my vision to right itself, I begin to hear gleeful laughter falling from the treetops of a walnut orchard nearby. The laughing stops as someone leaps out of a tree and lands with a light thud a short distance away. Quiet footsteps bring with them the intoxicating aroma of lavender, mint, and lemongrass, and I manage to smile as the presence begins to speak:

"Iris! Iris – a rainbow burned at midnight!
Why have your colors faded - all of them, but red?
Iris! Iris! Bleeding in the moonlight!
How could he do this to you – any worse, you would be...dead..."

Her tinkling voice trails off. Sniffling, she wraps her hand around three of my fingers and cries softly on my shoulder.

"Carya," I say. "Carya, it's good to see you." I realize that I can't see Carya at all, and yet my imagination paints her beautifully in my mind's eye... a teenaged girl clothed in robes dyed blue like a deep sea's waves...a coronet of pearls atop a head of waist-long auburn waves...sky-blue eyes that shimmer with starlight and purest tears.

I met her when I was just eleven, and felt like I was looking at an older sister. My hair is auburn like hers, but instead of wavy and full, it is board straight, pitifully thin, and reaches just below my ears. Acheron chopped it all off one night while he was drunk, and afterwards laughed at how boyish and ugly I looked, "sure to be a spinster, should I ever grant you the opportunity to marry," he said. My eyes, though blue like Carya's, are not blue like the sky's, at least not always. I'm told they change from looking light as the noonday sky to dark as dusk, depending on my mood. I haven't seen them sky-blue in years. Carya is also small-boned and thin like me, but I imagine she has more muscle than one might guess, like I do.

Carya is a nymph, immortal for all I can tell. She and dozens of others like her populate the dazzling stories of gods and heroes that captivate the wide-eyed youth of Petros. But all children grow up and learn to question the magic, the mystery, the myths they once loved so much, the princesses and warriors they wished to become. Even I believed the nymphs to be mere inventions of blind poets and bored sailors...until I was met face to face with Carya.

My vision slowly returning, I can see Carya untying a round silk pouch from her belt. I reach my hand into my own girdle and search for my jasper stone, something Carya gave to me the night I met her and that I've kept close to me ever since. But my hand resurfaces empty.

"Why did you give it to me? The stone I keep under my bed?" I say breathlessly, hoping with all my heart that the only possession I have in the world is safe within my chamber.

"Shhhh..." she replies, and then dips her fingers into her pouch, places the contents in her palm, and then spits into it.

"Now is not the time to ask questions, but to mend.
I was not sent to linger, but to your wounds attend."

I don't persist, perhaps because I know that doing so will have no effect on this unflappable creature, or perhaps because my master has taught me well never to challenge those in authority. As Carya nudges me to lie prostrate on the ground, I wonder why it is I'm allowing a thirteen year-old girl to have her way so easily. After all, I'm older than her now.

As I feel Carya fold up my tunic, I begin to rock from side to side and kick my feet defiantly, like a toddler refusing medicine. But the mixture of herbs and saliva she applies to my back and legs all but paralyzes me with instantaneous relief, and I remember that Carya is something much more than a girl, much more than an Alpha or Eusebian.

"New skin, perfect and pink, like the rosy dawn tomorrow,
In time you can be healed of your doubts, your fears, your sorrow."

It starts to rain and Carya lifts me up effortlessly, and I follow her eyes as they look directly above us where the Moonbow now hangs, its omniscient eye now illuminating each delicate raindrop.

"Jasper, red as blood and Moonbow's highest band,
Carry Jasper with you in your heart and in your hand.
Remember the bow still shines after darkest days are done.
Remember hope will follow you into bright orange desert sun."

Lowering my eyes to meet hers, I see only the walnut trees standing still as sentries at their posts. For a minute longer, I let them protect me, and let the Moonbow fill me with the foreign feeling of hope.

Hope. The word means nothing to a slave. But to a slave who is also a child of Asher, it means everything.

———

I make it to the Okeanos River without a single twinge of pain and leap eagerly to the water's edge where I have my fill of the sweet, untroubled stream. Then I remove my sandals and sit on the bank, trying to ignore the fragrance of Carya's remedy still seeping into my skin, and the sheen of the river reminding me of the Moonbow's presence.

Wiggling my toes in the water, I hear a loud splash upset the waves, followed by another...and another... and another... To my left, I count six people reveling in the moonlit ripples and spot two others standing guard close by on the shore– all of them likely bandits and orphans, given their tattered clothes, young, boisterous voices, and the undercurrent of defiance that fills them.

I can't help but look up to the Moonbow and whisper Carya's name, wishing she would appear one more time and tell me if I'll receive the doma or not. If I'm still a legitimate heir despite the distance I've kept between myself and Duna.

For a moment, I imagine myself joining these outlaws right here and now. Smashing Acheron's water jar against the trunk of the nearest willow tree and stomping the shards to pieces beneath my feet. Waking up each morning never knowing where or how I'll feed myself that day, or where I'll sleep at night. Forgetting my name and accepting a new one, or none at all. And letting the memories of my family, my home, and my childhood become dim and disjointed, like the fragments of irretrievable dreams.

The Moonbow is fading, and so is my patience with myself as I entertain daydreams of a different life, a coward's life; I cannot simply run away, not as long as my master still breathes.

I banish Carya and the doma to the dungeon of my mind and get to my feet, dragging the water pot with me. I turn to dip the jar into the river, but a bone-crushing grip seizes my shoulder, and I know... I'm not going anywhere.

CHAPTER THREE
AMBUSH

My other arm is swiftly clenched, and I'm spun around so fast that I drop Acheron's pot, sending it rolling toward the river. I try to yank myself free, desperate to jump after it, but my efforts are useless; my captor is a Giant, nearly twice my height and with more strength than all of his friends combined, I'm certain.

"No use getting soaked over a little water jug now, is there?" he says, watching me seethe as the jar glides onto the waves.

"It was my master's," I growl through gritted teeth.

The Giant shakes his head mockingly, making a sympathetic clicking noise with his tongue until the wandering object finds its way into the hands of one of the bathing bandits who holds it up triumphantly, then signals to us with the harsh call of a heron.

"I'll be dead in the morning if I return without it," I say, jerking fiercely in a foolish effort to salvage my only chance of survival.

My captor tightens his grip and grins at me like a lion with a mouse trapped under its paw. "Who's to say we won't kill you tonight...*Iris...*?"

Every muscle in my body tenses as I watch the four outlaws in the Okeanos swim toward us, alerted to the smell of fresh meat. These must be the rebels – the heathen rats – Acheron warned me about during tonight's bloody chastisement.

"How do you know my name?" I ask, silently cursing Carya for deserting me, leaving me with nothing more than worthless riddles and a mended body, ripe for breaking again.

"Being an orphan doesn't make you invisible. We've seen you in the marketplace. A sad lonely Eusebian girl we thought dead long ago, like her brother..."

The Giant releases me and withdraws into the shadows as the others encircle me, their helpless prey.

"Duna smiles on us!" shouts their leader, a wild-eyed, tan-skinned young man no older than me with a shaven head and a ragged scar on either cheek. Pacing toward me, he drops the water jar, sending it skidding to my feet. Staring at it stunned, I hear the Giant shout:

"Aren't you going to pick it up? After all, it belongs to your *beloved master!*" The din of jeering this incites is nearly deafening. Pressing my forefingers firmly against each ear, I can think of nothing else to do but yell back.

"He is not my beloved master!" I scream, vocal cords straining. The leader strikes his hand sideways through the air, silencing his pack. "I am a slave. I – "

"I know who you are. A wretched slave to the Guardian Acheron, yes. But more than that. You are the sister to a far more important man. A man who died honorably for his people," the leader says, unsheathing a small knife from his belt. "You'll soon find out if he finds *you* honorable."

The leader charges me, his iron blade poised to kill within seconds. I do as I did on countless – *needless* – occasions under Acheron's roof: draw a deep breath in and squeeze my eyes shut until I see tiny specks and swirls swimming behind my eyelids. *At least this will be over sooner than a whipping,* I think.

No sound is heard, only that of my heart beat begging for mercy. But I won't speak up on its behalf; if Carya hasn't arrived to plead for my life by now and the doma continues to elude me, then who am I to question whether my destiny is to die right here at the reckless hands of miscreants.

All at once I hear the low rumble of thunder, smell the sweetness of Juniper trees, feel the cool kiss of a raindrop on my temple – one last sensation before I'm killed and a pool of orphan blood stretches like a shadow into the life-giving river...

"Wait!" The voice does not belong to Carya. I open my eyes to see the outlaw leader frozen mid-stride, like a prowling wolf alerted to the sound of another rivaling huntsman. I can see him bristling.

Another man steps into the circle, stopping in between me and my newfound adversary. "What is it, Tycho! You're supposed to be standing guard!" the leader yells, his tanned face reddening with rage.

"Can we not use this girl, Lysander?" The protester speaks in a loud whisper, as if trying to keep his motive secret, as if I might dissent were I to hear it.

Before I can consider why this stranger is intervening – and more than that, whether I want him to – he turns abruptly and shoots me a look, interrupting my thoughts with dark eyes, stern and unreadable. As he comes closer to me I see clearly why he's been assigned the role of watchman. Though not a Giant like the guard whose hands could have snapped my arms like twigs, Tycho is broad-shouldered and tall, towering over his superior who glares up at him like a spoiled child. If circumstances were different, I might smile envisioning Tycho throwing the boy onto the opposite bank like a discus. But instead of smiling, I squint, making out the grotesque tattoo of a spotted serpent curled up on the underside of Tycho's right forearm, signifying sworn allegiance to Python, the only real god the Alphas and Eusebians agree exists.

I've heard some say that the gods and goddesses of the Alpha myths are as alive as we are, but that they were overthrown by Python millennia ago and enchained deep within the bowels of Petros. If this is true, I wonder why Carya and her kind have not been captured as well. Perhaps that explains why she isn't here now; she fears Tycho would carry her away into the heart of the Great Sea to be sacrificed into the waves of the underworld...

"Would you kill Acheron?" I jump at Tycho's words. The idea of killing my master thrills me, and yet I stand speechless. *How would I do it...*

"Answer him, Iris!" commands Lysander, obviously consenting to his guard's clever suggestion.

"I...I...I'm not..." My words catch in my throat.

The leader lets out a slow impatient sigh while the six outlaw-dogs around him begin to snarl.

"Kill her! Kill her, Lysander!" I hear one howl. "Acheron will have us all strapped to pyres within a week if you don't!" The other outlaws shake their fists and shout in agreement as Lysander tosses his knife from hand to hand, back and forth, back and forth, back and forth...

The images conjured by the mention of Enochos are enough to loosen my tongue and unshackle my feet; no Eusebian, no matter how malignant, will burn there because of me. I step forward, and the riot and Lysander's restlessness die down until all I hear is the far-off screech of a Barn Owl.

"Acheron will have us all killed sooner or later..." I begin.

Before the bandits' muttering can reach a murderous crescendo, Lysander whispers into Tycho's ear.

"Let her speak!" Tycho bellows. Lysander whistles for the Giant and quickly points at me with his knife.

Moments later the sentry is looming over my shoulder, and my second chance is granted with a curt nod of Lysander's head. "Choose your words carefully, girl," he says, his knife still staring at my heart. I touch my chest nervously and turn to face away from the ready weapon.

"I said Acheron will have us killed because he hates Eusebians more than anything. The only reason I am still alive is because Acheron takes pleasure in punishing me," I say.

The only reason Niobe is still alive is because he delights in deceiving her, speaking tenderly to her, coddling her until she believes he truly loves her. But what he truly adores is hearing her sob until sunrise after he tells her she holds as much worth as the entrails of the swine she cooked for his supper.

I decide not to mention Niobe, hoping she will be spared from a similar ambush of her own.

"He was the one who ordered my brother's execution three years ago," I continue. "Five Eusebians were burned alive because they were servants of the high priest. Because they begged Acheron to stop the pagans from sacrificing in the Temple – "

"And your master demanded one-hundred thousand drachmae from the Temple treasury instead," Tycho interjects. "When Eirene got word of it, the whole city sent a beggar's basket around on his behalf."

"To raise money for the poor, poor Alpha Guardian..." Lysander chimes in with a thespian's lamenting wail.

"Acheron couldn't stand being made a mockery of," Tycho finishes the story, the one I would die a hundred times to rewrite and bring my brother back. I look up at him. Able to read his eyes this time, I see in them what I have not perceived in a mortal's face for years...compassion. "I am sorry, I – "

"Sorry? Why are you sorry?" Lysander interrupts crossly. "You had nothing to do with it. The only one who should be sorry is *her* as long as she continues to wash the feet and take the lashes of her brother's murderer!" He lunges toward me and laughs as I shrink back from the knife like a tendril from winter's touch. "What is your answer, slave!"

"I will kill him," I whisper.

"Speak louder!" shouts Lysander.

"I will kill him!" I exclaim. As I shout, I feel familiar tingling in my veins again, and seconds later, the same burning arrows I felt coursing through me the night Jasper died, only worse. Much, much worse.

I feel every eye on me, each one waiting to watch me try in vain to run away or recant my declaration. But the heat grows hotter and settles in the palms of my hands. "Stop…" I whisper to myself. "Calm down." I take a deep breath, but it does no good. My hands feel like they're going to explode. I cry out in pain and shake my arms as though they're covered with vicious bees.

"What's wrong with her?" I hear someone say.

"She's crazed! Look at her hands!" shouts another.

I look down at my palms. They're glowing orange with fire. The tips of my fingers are red as irons in a furnace.

"It's a doma," Lysander whispers. He lowers his knife and carefully backs away from me.

I turn toward the river and violently try to throw the fire out of my hands.

It works. Two fireballs, the size of my fists, sizzle and hiss through my skin, then soar through the air, arcing over the water like shooting stars and landing with a crackling roar in the center of a Juniper's trunk.

"You're an Asher!" Lysander says with an awe-struck grin spreading across his face. "Why didn't you say so?"

I blow on my hands and look up at the dumbfounded faces staring back at me. "I didn't know I had the gift. Until now."

I feel like I've just stepped into a dream. To be sure it isn't, I turn and look back at the fire burning across the river. The Juniper has become a lantern flickering in the darkness.

"Looks like you have your chance. To have your vengeance," says Lysander.

He looks up into a shaft of morning light piercing though the armor of trees around us, then fiercely throws his dagger into a willow ten yards away. "Another gift for you," he says pointing after it.

With a whistle, he sends all of the outlaws scattering into the remaining shadows. He starts after them, but turns, remembering something. I gasp as I watch him punt Acheron's water pot into the middle of the river. "Don't worry, Iris. He won't need it anymore," he smiles.

⸺◅०/०/०⤙⸺

I hasten back to Enochos, hoping to make it to Acheron's house before both daylight and reason catch up with me and pull this knife from my shaking fist, forcing me to stop and consider this newfound power. As I run, I wonder how I created the fire at Okeanos. Was it formed as a response to feeling threatened? Angry? Afraid?

In my mind's eye I replay my brother's pyre going up in flames, then Acheron's drunken grin flashing in the smoke. Hot needles prick my skin from the inside, sending streams of heat from the tops of my shoulders all the way down to my knuckles. *That's it...Hate.*

I soundlessly push my way into the courtyard surrounding Acheron's house through a small door, the one nearest the entrance into the andron where he spends most of his time, listening to poets, hosting a symposium, punishing his slaves... It is where I left him last night, locked in a slumber of wine and wickedness, unwittingly drawing his last breaths.

I pull my cloak over my head and make my way to an open window where I crouch and wait for my breathing to slow and my heart rate to settle. I can't lose control. Not now. It feels as if time has stopped, standing still just long enough to see the slave girl become an assassin.

I step into the andron and approach a crumpled body lying upon the mosaic River Styx. A body whose head has blond hair that's been unevenly cut by Acheron's knife. I run to her, to Niobe, but I'm too late. A whip is wrapped tightly around her lifeless throat.

CHAPTER FOUR
HUNTER

I try to summon the fire. I want to burn down this place and incinerate every trace of Acheron's existence. I feel the heat inside me, beating in my heart, burning in my lungs, but it isn't the same. I turn my hands over and see only pink flesh still cooling from their exhibition at Okeanos. I grit my teeth, close my eyes, and flex every muscle in my body, trying so hard to conjure the doma that I make myself lightheaded.

Why isn't it working?

I wander back into the courtyard, every muscle cramping, my head swimming, and slide down the rough mud brick wall, and weep for Niobe.

After what feels like hours, I open my eyes and watch the pale blue haze of morning light creep closer, like an ominous Enochos wave. Suddenly I feel as though I'm back in that icy sea and that at any moment, Acheron, the gallant

Guardian, will hook his arm around my flailing body and force me onto shore. Only this time, he will not view me as a harmless, able-bodied slave girl worth saving, but as an expendable, untrustworthy Eusebian deserving death.

I wonder what Niobe did to provoke him; it could have been anything. Perhaps she spent one too many minutes ridding the mosaic river of my blood, or spoke heedlessly of the Oracles and the Moonbow's promise as she did three years ago. The next possibility makes my blood run cold...

Could it be that Niobe spoke in my defense, once again wrongly believing she had won his favor and the right to speak freely? I never considered Niobe a friend. She resented any woman to whom Acheron showed affection, whether actual or pretended, especially one whose life he'd saved. But she was no enemy either. Had she been, what would have prevented her from slipping hemlock or mandrake into my soup the night I was brought in, brain and body numb from hypothermia? I was on the edge of death, and she chose to pull me away from it. What would have kept her from whispering lies about me into Acheron's ear, feeding his suspicions that I had been corrupted with revolutionary ideas?

When I was helpless, bleeding on the floor, she didn't look on with satisfaction. She fled the room, aghast at the sight of her sister Eusebian suffering at the hands of a charming tyrant. I'm almost sure of it. Niobe had allowed her mind to rip the mask from Acheron's face, revealing the coldness of his eyes, the poison of his silver tongue, the cruelty of his kiss.

I hear the wooden gate creak open and the rustling of the groundskeepers as they enter to begin another day, just as they did yesterday and the day before, and the day before that. Alphas all of them, they've never known suffering at Acheron's hand; they've merely stood by stoically and watched his wrath fall, hard and sporadic like hail from a thunderhead, before returning to their precious pomegranate trees and dainty trellises of bougainvillea. I try not to despise them. It isn't their fault that I am Eusebian, *"a daughter of Duna,"* and they are Alpha, children of a petty pantheon of lost immortals who have inherited their ancestors' lust for power.

Before the servants notice me and, I fear, report my whereabouts to Acheron, I navigate around the house on hands and knees until I am well hidden beneath the shade and foliage of a flowering myrtle.

Clip-clop, clip-clop, clip-clop. My heartbeat mimics the sharp staccato rhythm of horse hooves pounding the cobblestone path outside the wall. I know only one person who travels on horseback.

"Good morning, Darius," I hear Acheron say, using a sickeningly blithe tone only an unfeeling murderer could be capable of after strangling a slave. "I've been called to Eirene for the day. Clean up the mess inside after you've pruned the olive trees, and tell the girl to wait for me in the andron when she returns."

I don't linger another moment. I make my way, low like a lizard, to the entrance nearest the slaves' quarters and quietly trespass into the chamber I shared with Niobe. The pungent smell of leeks, onions, and celery simmered together fills my nostrils, and I feel my belly begin to ache for it. As I survey the room in search of the food, a flash of red catches my eye.

There, shimmering in a sliver of sunlight upon a bronze spoon, is my jasper stone. I must have dropped it during my nightmare last night. Acheron had strict rules about slaves' possessions. The only things we were allowed to keep were the clothes on our backs and sandals on our feet. The jasper stone, luckily, was small enough to fit inside my sandal while I worked and stay wrapped under my fingers as I slept.

I fall down before the tiny red rock as though it were a recovered relic atop a temple altar, then carefully draw it to my heart.

"That's the last time I leave you behind," I swear to it. And then I begin to cry again when I think of Niobe, whom I also left behind. I try to tell myself that there was nothing I could do to stop Acheron from killing her. Nothing, that is, without the doma.

If only I had received it last night! My eyes burn with tears once more. "I could have stopped him... I could have *killed* him!" I nearly shout.

In the corner of the room, below the window and away from the light, is the lentil soup contained in one of Acheron's finest black bowls.

It depicts two persimmon-colored women standing at an upright loom, busy turning raw wool into cloth. I hold the lukewarm vessel to my face and take in its earthy aroma, then fetch the spoon and gingerly dip it into the broth. As I bring the spoon to my lips, I notice a crabbed inscription etched vertically into the bowl above a basket full of yarn: ἀδελφός...*Sisters.*

Niobe, my Eusebian sister, is nourishing me, bringing my soul and body back to life as she did before; but this time with intangible sustenance far more invigorating than lentil soup alone. Clasping the jasper stone and filling my belly with her final gift, I resolve that every fiber and thread of my life will be woven with one unwavering purpose – to watch Acheron melt head to foot in the volcanic heat from my hands.

⟞⟨3/3/3⟩⟝

The fever is ready to release my mother's broken body from its torturous hands – one ice-cold, the other fire-hot. My brother surrendered to sleep hours ago, but I stay close by her bed near the window, trusting the moonlight to keep me awake.

As if spiraling down from the ceiling above us, a cool breeze sweeps through the room, and at once I feel peace settle upon me like a mantle. My mother's groaning ceases completely; was it not for a smile appearing on her pale, cracked lips, I would think her dead.

Lifting my eyes from hers, still closed, I see something peculiar forming low in the midnight sky. First, a faint arc of silvery light with a misty sheet of rain falling through it, then seven transparent ribbons of color materializing one by one beneath the first. I close an eye and hold my thumb and forefinger to the bow, creating a frame around the portrait, perfectly aglow with brushstrokes, barely golden.

If only I could pull it into the room with us and let my mother hold it, just for a while, I thought.

"*Mother...*" I whispered, as if a tone any louder would chase away the Moonbow, or worse, dissolve the serenity it was casting over us.

"*Iris...*" I felt the color escape my face as I turned to see the source of a young girl's voice, just like mine only sweetened with poetry.

There she is, a goddess-like nymph standing in the room's single shaft of light, arrayed in royal robes and the soothing scents of springtime herbs. She takes a step toward me and smiles up at the Moonbow. Somehow, I know without question that this intruder is a friend.

" *... Iris, Child of the Rainbow,*
I am Carya, sent by Duna. I've known you from afar.
Take heart, Iris, gaze upon the Moonbow,
Your mother flies beyond it, passed the furthest star.
Hear me, she is well now, free from fever's pain,
A promise for you, Iris: you can be with her again."

The nymph spends the rest of the night kneeling at my side, sometimes weeping with me, other times softly humming. All the while, I struggle to let my mother go, battling to believe her spirit has soared through the Moonbow's arches as Carya has promised.

As the sunrise climbs out of the distant hills, Carya embraces me and places a smooth red jasper stone in my hand, whispering:

"*Red, the color of courage, of passion, strength, and love.*
Jasper will point the way to the Moonbow's light above."

Before my lips can part to ask the meaning of the strange gift, Carya has already vanished.

After the sun finishes transforming the Moonbow into ordinary sky, Jasper walks in and takes Carya's place beside me. He folds his arms on the bed and buries his head into them, sobbing. Not sure what else to do, I do what Carya did and cry alongside him.

"Why didn't you wake me?" Jasper asks just as the morning chorus of birds stops singing.

I can't speak. My focus is fixed on the emptiness of the indigo horizon.

Noticing my restless fingers rubbing Carya's stone between them, Jasper sighs with pity. "Remember what mother said, Iris. It isn't over."

"Did you see her?" I ask him before I lose my courage.

"Who?"

"The girl. Carya. She was just here before you came in. I think she's a goddess, Jasper."

"You were just imagining, sister," he says. The time he takes to think about his words tells me he feels sorry for me. "Our minds... Well, they can play tricks on us. And there's no such thing as goddesses. Those are just made-up Alpha stories."

"No, Jasper!" I say, gripping his wrist, not wanting to be talked to like a child. "She's real. She gave me this." I hold out my other hand for him to see the stone. "It's jasper, like the ones we used to find on the beach."

Jasper sighs and scratches his forehead. "We have boxes full of those, Iris." He lowers his hand and wraps his arm around my shoulder, drawing me into his side. "I love you. I thank Duna we can comfort one another."

Of course. He thinks I've taken a stone from our collection and have fancied it an enchanted keepsake from a mythical goddess.

As Jasper gently takes our mother from the bed, I swear never to speak another word to him about Carya – partly because I don't want to be thought crazy, and partly because I fear that I am.

I'm startled awake by the strident screech of a hawk flying somewhere above me. I squeeze my hand around the jasper stone and carefully roll onto my back, which feels significantly better that it did last night...thanks to Carya. "See, Jasper. I'm not crazy," I speak to the sky, hoping my brother hears me.

My eyes flutter open to see a vulture pecking at a carcass just an arm span from where I lie. I jump to my feet and amble toward a small ravine, lest it think that I, too, am something to be scavenged.

I trudged all morning through the rocky hills enclosing Enochos until my wearied legs refused to take me any farther. *When I kill him, I will also take his horse.* I smile at the thought. At the rate I'm traveling, it could be weeks before I make it to the Eusebian city of Limén where I hope to find work. If I want to kill Acheron, I will have to keep myself alive, and I don't want to steal or kill for food if I can help it.

I peer into the stream and scan the face looking back at me. No longer a vulnerable orphan or a defenseless slave, I see the capricious visage of a liar, a thief, a fugitive, and yes... an *assassin.* I will become anything I must in order to avenge my brother and the other innocents who have died to satisfy Acheron's black-hearted whims. And I won't need the doma to help me.

I hear a low-pitched growl and watch the water waken with ripples creeping across it from the opposite shore. My gaze leaves my reflection's eyes and meets those of a gray wolf; his slight yet powerful paws have already begun advancing toward me. It is easy to judge from his long, scrawny limbs and protruding ribcage that he won't leave any part of me behind for the vultures...if he has his way.

He stops seven feet from me, standing stiff-legged and tall. When he sees me reach for my knife, he crouches and curls up his lips, revealing six sharp incisors ready to tear open my throat.

Staring into the wolf's golden eyes, I try to imagine that I am face to face with Acheron. I anticipate the thrill of walking away from his dead body without turning back. No regrets.

The passing of a cloud over the midday sun sends a shadow over our battleground, and a swell of confidence through my body. I initiate the charge with a long lunge and an extended hand tipped with the solitary blade, daring my enemy to attack. He points his ears and barks quietly, perhaps humored by my modest display of bravery. In the next second, he is six feet in the air and my arm is outstretched as high as it can reach. Every muscle and sinew in me remains rigid and unmoving as I wait with suspended breath and unblinking eyes for the animal to descend.

As the darkness of his body falls over me, I thrust my dagger up into his underbelly, and together we collapse into the shallow riverbed. I lock eyes with the beast as his eyes soften and mouth closes. He whimpers as I retract the knife and roll him off of my chest.

Though my father was a tanner, we never saw the animals alive. I've never killed anything...at least not on purpose. Years ago I once hurled a spotted stone at the nest of two barn swallows I'd found under a bridge near my family's house, curious to see if the mother bird might sit upon it like one of her eggs. The rock struck her glossy blue wing and she warbled wildly until her male companion joined her side. All at once, as though I'd been buried by an avalanche propelled by my own voice, I felt what it was to regret.

Overwhelmed with shame, I ran home as fast I could, my throat tightening as I tried in vain to restrain a surge of tears. Jasper could barely understand me as I begged him, in between heavy, inconsolable sobs, to bandage the broken wing.

"You must be careful, Iris. Had she been a larger animal, she would've defended herself, and then *you* might have been the one in need of mending," Jasper warned with a facetious smile. But there was truth in what he said, and I thought to myself I wouldn't harm another creature unless it first threatened me.

I'm glad I don't have to stab the wolf again. Within a few seconds, his whimpering stops and his belly stops rising. I drag him by the hind legs onto shore, then walk back down to the water and wash my hands and knife.

Before I leave, I peer into the water. And though it's unrecognizable at first, I know the face looking back at me by the pain and weariness that encircle its dark blue eyes. It's the face of the woman I will be until my journey is done – this is *Hunter.*

CHAPTER FIVE
RUNAWAY

By nightfall I make it to the Port of Ourania. Unlike Enochos, home to the executioner's lonely vessel and the few combustible pyres of criminals, Ourania's waters are crowded with cargo ships and fishing boats bringing everything from wood and wheat to squid and silver into the arms of the bustling harbor. Only a half circle of sun sits on the soft, flame-orange horizon, and yet sailors and dockworkers scurry like nocturnal ants, carrying load after load to and from their assigned crafts.

I stop and sit on an empty crate and heave the dead wolf off of my burning shoulders. I've been tempted countless times to stop and skin him, making my journey easier, but I talked myself out of it, thinking it wise to keep him as he is so that I can handily prove my skill when I find a tanner to work for. I also hope that it can serve as a reminder – to myself and to others – that I can fend for myself.

Setting my limp and lifeless trophy on the ground, I'm suddenly struck by a nausea that feels strangely like sea sickness, and I realize I've traveled nearly fifteen miles today with nothing more than Niobe's lentil soup to keep me moving.

"You must be starved!"

My empty stomach leaps into my throat as I jump at the deep voice calling to me. I hear the stranger chuckle at my reaction, and as I turn angrily to face the irritant, I'm met with the likeness of a hideous serpent stained into the olive skin of a muscular forearm. I follow its forked tongue up to the familiar face of Tycho, the outspoken outlaw who found it prudent to deem me a Guardian's killer.

"I didn't mean to startle you, my lady," he says, his smile fading at the sight of my furrowed brow framing exhausted eyes.

I look over my shoulder, then back at Tycho with a feeble shrug.

"Expecting someone?" he asks.

"No. I was looking for this lady you speak of," I joke, with immediate regret. I can't let this stranger get too close. He's a Pythonian who has seen the doma I possess. It could be very valuable to him...

"What else am I to call you? Artemis, Goddess of the Hunt?" he says, pointing at the dead wolf at my feet.

"That's funny. Most people believe that I was named to honor the rainbow goddess." *Most...except for Jasper...*

My gaze drifts out to sea, and with my mind I create a faraway world of the wine-dark water, remembering the day I first beat Jasper in a hundred-yard foot race through a field of wildflowers.

"I'd say you are swifter than Iris of the Rainbow, sister!" he'd exclaimed, hands on his knees as he caught his breath.

I watched as his earnest eyes searched the multi-colored meadow beneath us until they settled on a favorite; he picked a purple flower from

the earth, shook off the dirt, and examined the specimen proudly. "Now...
this is what you are named for," he said, tucking the Iris blossom behind
my ear. "All of the beauty of the rainbow bursting out of one little girl, just
like papa said."

"I don't think much of the gods, my lady. But you've got a pretty flower
named for you." My reverie is shattered as I jump once more at Tycho's
words. Does this Pythonian know my thoughts?

"I don't mean to scare you." He pauses, as if contemplating how he might
ease my nerves, and then extends his right hand for me to grasp. I stand to
take it, trying not to focus on the python's beady black eyes staring up at me
from Tycho's arm. "Don't mind him, my lady. He doesn't bite," he jests with
a broad, dimpled grin that I can't help but find disarming.

I check myself, recalling the countless times I was warned as a child
never to fraternize with a Pythonian:

"Beware the venom of the Pythonian mark."

It is said that the dark god's disciples can be as quick to draw blood as
they are to offer aid. I think of Tycho interceding on my behalf, stopping
Lysander from sending me to the River Styx to join Niobe as her soul floated
toward an afterlife I'm terrified to face. He offered help, even saved my life,
and now he slithers onto my path again, full of wiles and lethal fangs.

"You're a servant of Python. It's *your* bite I should be wary of," I say,
lowering my hand and returning to my seat. Tycho's eyes turn with sadness
to the sea, and I wonder what troubling memory the quiet waves conjure
in his mind's eye, what depth of evil his devotion to Python has led him to.

"You think I don't know what your tattoo means? I want nothing to do
with you," I announce tersely. Hoisting the wolf around my shoulders, I
turn and make for the nearest cargo ship, one being filled with bushels of
barley, beans, dates and figs.

"Wait!" Tycho's voice shouts the word with the same measure of
boldness and desperation it possessed one day ago, when it seized Lysander

and prevented an orphan's homicide. He was determined to keep me alive then, and now I sense it was purely to advance a nefarious mission, perhaps to sacrifice my doma to his god, or offer me as a priestess to be clothed in white and stripped of virtue.

I stop and stand still for a minute, spending every second of it listening to the logic that scolds my halted feet and urges me to keep walking, to forget this Odysseus, this sly deceiver, and hurry onto the boat before he can utter another word. But I turn in spite of myself, ready to spit out the honeyed words he'll speak, to avert my eyes should he flash a smile that would put handsome Achilles to shame.

But he doesn't speak. He doesn't smile. He only skims the sand with his topaz eyes and begins twisting his left hand around his tattooed forearm, as if trying to strangle the ineffaceable serpent.

"I may have to chop off this arm," he says, giving a half-hearted laugh. I return his good humor with a frown and expel a dissatisfied sigh.

"I renounced my vows to Python nearly a decade ago. I give you my word," Tycho says, the deep timbre of his voice pleading with me to believe him.

Discerning the suspicion on my face, he continues. "I was – *am* – a Eusebian also. Perhaps not an orthodox one," he laughs. "I always wanted to know more about good and evil and where it all came from, to go deeper, beyond what the old stories tell us. I guess you could say it got me into trouble – for a while, at least."

Not caring to hear Tycho's testimony of prodigality, nor about any spiritual epiphany, I take a deep breath and look restlessly toward the ship.

"And like your brother," Tycho continues, changing the subject to appease me, "I wanted a better life for our people, wanted to do everything in my power to drive the Petrodians out of Eirene and win our freedom."

"What power?" I say, unable to keep the snide remark from sliding off my tongue.

"Exactly, my lady. I had none. I have no doma," he jokes. I must not look amused because he clears his throat and proceeds as though he never mentioned my gift. "But I found someone who claimed to have all the power in the world," Tycho says. "And he was willing to give me access to it if I only served him and accepted his mark." He releases his forearm and looks past me to the cargo ship. "It's getting dark. That trading ship is headed to Limén. And it appears to be carrying plenty of food. Was I right when I said you must be hungry?" I nod. My stomach churns, and I begin to salivate as I imagine biting into the sweet, pulpy flesh of a fresh ripe fig.

"I'm famished," I reply, feeling my empty stomach twist itself into an intolerable knot, punishing me for neglecting it so long.

Tycho approaches me and lifts the dead wolf from my back and places it on his own. "Come on then, my lady. We can use your friend here to pay our way!"

"I can't sell the wolf," I say, my voice losing strength with every breath. "I have to use it to get work."

"You can't get work without having some food first," Tycho reasons. "And there will be other wolves for you to kill."

His smile slams the door on a likely trap, and I follow him to the dock. Even if I am being led away to be made a slave again, I am too tired to turn away for caution's sake, too hungry to care.

The captain was pleased to accept the wolf carcass in return for passage and supper aboard his ship. He laughed that I had not skinned it yet, but I didn't mind; I was simply glad to be rid of the weight and stench of it. The helmsmen greeted Tycho like they were all old friends, and indeed, they seemed to regard him as one of their own and promptly enlisted him to help ready the oars and sails. Before they could ask me any questions, I sneaked away to the bow like a stowaway and ate voraciously of olives and figs until my stomach could hold no more.

Groaning, I lie back on the boat and rest my hands on a full belly. Staring up at an ill-boding blanket of cloud cover, I feel reason and good sense returning to me, and I silently scream to myself:

How weak you are! You've joined yourself to a Pythonian, and perhaps a whole ship of them. If you die tonight, no one could say you didn't deserve it.

"Please, Tycho...don't tell us that pretty girl you brought along is your sister..." I hear one say.

"She's mine if she isn't!" another shouts.

My cheeks begin to burn with both embarrassment and rage, and I rise to hear what Tycho might say.

"Yes. She is my sister," he answers. "And she'll be treated with respect."

Grumbling and laughter emanate from the deck as the sailors assure him no harm will come to me, then go on about their business until finally oars are grasped and Poseidon prayed to for safe voyage, a ritual of superstitious sailors, no matter their religion.

Moments later, Tycho taps me on the shoulder. "You can sleep in there," he says, pointing to a small tent two yards behind me. I must appear dubious because he crouches to me and adds, "I'll be right here. No one will bother you. I'll wake you when we're in Limén."

"I can take care of myself," I say, wishing my hands would warm just enough for him to see them glow.

"All right, then," is all he says.

I wait a few minutes after he leaves, then settle into the sackcloth shelter. Quickly, I am lulled to sleep by the ship at sea before regret can collapse this cocoon of safety, as fleeting as it may be.

CHAPTER SIX
LIMÉN

onight my dreams are spared from the pyres of Enochos. In its place, the Alpha tale of an ill-fated goddess lifts itself from somewhere deep within my psyche, from a forgotten fragment of my childhood spent beside my Alpha schoolmates who danced and sang her story as if it were a wedding march. It's the legend of Persephone, one of Zeus's daughters whose beauty caught the lustful eye of Hades, god-king of the underworld.

> " ... He wanted her as his queen, and he called to her by name.
> Beside the glowing narcissus, she plucked irises of blue,
> And when his chariot rode past her, their dainty petals flew ... "

After Persephone's abduction, her mother Demeter forbade the earth to produce its bounty. The world would hunger and wallow in winter as long as she was without the daughter she loved more than life itself, more than immortality...

"The seeds made stubborn did not grow; oxen curved their plows in vain,
Cruel famine brought no sacrifices, and priests' tears brought no rain.
When Zeus perceived this in his heart, he sent Iris down below,
But not even heaven's aid could melt Demeter's heart of snow."

Neither mighty Zeus nor Hades could contend with Demeter's wrath. But Hades could outwit her. Before he allowed his bride to be ushered back to the realm of mortals, he nourished her with fruit grown in sun-starved orchards, plucked by bloodless hands.

"But with the pomegranate seeds, Hades sealed her infernal reign,
For when spring wilts and cold winds blow, she is his queen again."

Persephone had seeds of hell itself inside her. And so she was destined to dwell below the earth for one third of the year. During her absence, the earth was forsaken, plagued with barrenness until the day she would emerge like a shining white lily in spring.

The dream wounds me with memories of a past that is not my own. I long for Persephone. I sense my soul reaching out to her as though she were Jasper upon the pyre. If I were a goddess, I would turn Petros into a bitter wasteland until he returned from the underworld. If Zeus truly did exist, I would implore him every hour of every day to intercede and end Hades's heartless reign before he could destroy another life or curse another world.

But Zeus does not exist. And Duna has been more foe than friend. At least the Alphas have come to see that their myths have no more substance than the funereal dreams of an orphan slave. My people insist their prophecies are true, that their deity cares for them. They gasp prayers into the air and swear that they are heard. Some, like Jasper, are so deeply deceived that they revere the Moonbow as a symbol of Phos' victory over Python in the Great Sea seven years ago.

In my dream, I look out through Demeter's eyes as she sways back and forth on an ocean of fading blue irises, a Narcissus petal from her daughter's hair dangling from her hand. I can feel her heart aching, eyes burning as her gaze penetrates the cloud cover. She is yearning to pray. She wants nothing more than to call upon heaven to save her from her misery. But she dares not; she knows nothing worthy of prayer lies beyond that wall of sky. Nothing could be more futile than waiting for answers from an unseen god or aid from his unknown army. So she will tear her eyes from Mount Olympus forever and exile herself to this gray, grief-stricken sea...

"Mighty Poseidon! Brother of Almighty Zeus! I beseech you! End this storm!"

The melody of my night song shatters as I awaken to the sound of the captain howling like a crazed wolf at the sky. I find myself in hazy twilight, trapped between slumber and the waking world as the shards of the myth continue to pierce me, and my eyes open up to another nightmare.

⸺◈◈◈⸺

I peek outside the tent as two great arms of lilac lightning seize the sea just a hundred yards from the ship. I wonder if Duna could see my dreams; perhaps he's punishing me for recanting the faith I followed blindly as a child.

Staring out into the storm with Demeter's stubbornness coursing through me, I stagger out of the tent onto slick wet wood to let the Eusebian god get a better look at his rebel orphan. I slip and fall several times as I make my way to the opposite edge of the boat. The thunder vibrates inside my chest as I watch rain, wind, and flashing light thrash against each other, pushing the wrathful waves ever closer to my clenched, unyielding hands. I hear the captain bark orders through the downpour and the frantic feet of the crew scurrying and sliding behind me. Some mutter curses, other shout out prayers, but the storm only grows fiercer.

"What do you think you're doing?!" Tycho takes me by the shoulders and pulls me away from my defiant perch.

I feel my tongue pressing hard into the roof of my mouth, fighting back a torrent of tears, and I cannot free it to offer him an answer. The truth is, I don't know what I'm doing. Only that I want to know why Duna has taken away everyone I love and why I'm still here, alive and alone with nothing but nightmares and a doma that is of no good to me.

"You'll die out here," Tycho grunts as he yanks me back by the wrist and in one swift motion throws me over his shoulder.

I kick and punch and scream and flail, but Tycho ignores me like a bull ignores a fly buzzing around its horns. And now, as a bounty hunter returning dutifully with his prisoner in tow, Tycho thrusts open the door to the captain's cabin, turns around, slides me off his back like a wet winter cloak, and sets me down on the last dry deck of the ship.

"Like I told you earlier, I'll wake you when we're in Limén," he says, shutting the door.

A few moments later, I crawl quietly toward the door, but am stopped by the sound of a key locking me in, keeping me safe from the roaring waves that tempt my wandering spirit.

<hr />

From under the door, a long faint line of yellow light points itself at me like the tip of a sword, and I cannot help but notice that even warm morning sunshine, welcomed by most, can remind me of death. I roll through the diaphanous blade, stretch my arms, and then remember where I am. I jump to my feet and begin pounding my fists against my prison door. Seconds later, I hear the key inside the lock, smell the salty air, and feel my lungs expand in longing for it.

Tycho opens the door and presents his palm, occupied by a plump, purple fig. He takes it in his other hand, twists off its stem and offers it to me, his idea of an olive branch, I assume.

"Never touch me again!" I yell. "I told you...I can take care of myself!" With that, I pinch the fig between my fingers, split it open, take a bite, and step out into a blinding brightness.

"The ugliest storms make the most beautiful mornings, don't they?" I hear Tycho say. *Did he even hear me shout at him?*

I slowly open my eyes and see the sailors busy unloading the ship and sweeping the deck, smiling and carrying on - last night's terror already long forgotten. "We arrived an hour ago. I thought it best to let you sleep a while longer." Tycho pats me on the shoulder, then jumps over the side of the ship and onto the dock. He pushes a wooden ramp against the ship and waits as I clumsily stumble down it.

"You'll have your sea legs soon enough," Tycho laughs.

Thanks to yours, I've lived to see another morning, I think, and I try to discern whether I feel grateful to him, or resentful. I suppose I will have to wait and see what Limén holds for me before I can be sure...

"I don't intend to board another boat again if I can help it," I say. I untie my sandals and carry my wobbly legs as fast I can toward the white, glowing shore, then plunge each foot into the sparkling sand and drop onto it like a child introducing herself to snow. I remove the jasper stone from my girdle and hold it up to the iris-colored sky. It fits there perfectly, a radiant red queen for the glorious gold sun.

I admire these regal spheres until a wind pushes a cloud across the sun. I lower my stone, reminded of Carya's last words to me:

"Remember hope will follow you into bright orange desert sun."

Has hope followed me here to Limén, this Eusebian land on the eastern edge of the desert wilderness?

Before I can begin to wonder what that meddlesome nymph might have meant with her riddle, Tycho drops my sandals at my side.

"What do you suppose you'll do now?" he asks.

I slip the stone back into its pouch and put on my sandals as I try to conceive a response that will relieve him of the curious pity he has for me.

"If you must know, I'm going to find work," I say, rising to my feet. Tycho searches my eyes, unsure of the confidence I'm trying hard to project with unblinking eyes, a slight upward tilt of my chin, and easy, even breaths. "As a tanner, like my father." Tycho looks down at his right arm, then back at me with eyes darkened by the unknown memories that lurk behind them.

"Your papa taught you well. Never trust Pythonians...no matter what they do," he says. He takes my left hand in his and leans over it with a kiss. "You'll be in my prayers, Iris."

I nod just once, and off he walks without another word.

As I watch him disappear into the crowd, I tremble and gaze at the dome of the desert sun. What if this Pythonian, my mysterious protector, was the "hope" of which Carya sang? If Duna does exist, and his messenger-nymph had indeed delivered a message to me, I have judged it wrongly, rejected it willfully, and cast it away without even saying thank you.

CHAPTER SEVEN
MESSENGER

I float aimlessly through Limén's streets like a disembodied spirit journeying along the Styx, but without the underworld ferryman to guide me to my destination, I don't know when or where to stop, and feel as though I might haunt this place forever. The streets are crowded with shouting merchants, braying donkeys being prodded and laden with goods, and busy slaves, some buying fine frocks of every shade, others honey-drizzled pastries, ceramic jugs of wine, and silk slippers.

The sight of shoes reminds me that I haven't been floating. On the contrary, I have walked more than twenty miles in a matter of days. I look down at my own dust-covered feet, my toenails caked with mud, and the deteriorating sandals that have rubbed raw my heels and ankles. I promise myself that the first thing I will do when I earn my first drachma is buy a sturdy pair of boots, the kind the actors wear in tragic plays to increase their stature.

The edge of town isn't far, I tell myself. *Just make it to a tannery. It won't be far...*

I continue on, one tiresome, sore step at a time until the sunlight's departure and the emergence of shadows awaken my consciousness; a few seconds later, the strong, familiar whiff of a dead animal gets my attention.

I turn to see an old man, a tanner no doubt, trudging slowly toward the street's lonely end, a mound of dried animal skins stacked on either shoulder. His hair is gray and nearly gone, his frame wiry, but not weak. As if sensing my furtive examination of him, the tanner turns slightly to the right, and I see a slight, twinkling eye that reminds me of my father's. Half-driven by my desperate need for food and work, half-driven to meet a man so much like my father, I hurry after him.

"Sir! Sir!" I call out, then join him at his side. He seems unsurprised by my sudden appearance and continues on at a steady pace, as if passing the time with an old friend.

"Hello, girl. Welcome to the city."

"Hello," I say slowly, mimicking the mellowness of his voice. "How did you know I'm not from Limén?"

"I've lived here all my sixty-eight years and walked up and down this street more times than I know how to count. Yours is the only strange face I know," he says, pausing to skim my face a few seconds to make certain it's foreign to him.

"Well it won't be strange to you any longer. My name is Iris. I'm a tanner's daughter from Eirene."

"A tanner, you say? Well, you're no stranger indeed," he says, eyebrows forming a pleasant arch around his sky-blue eyes. "I'm Gennadius, a tanner also. But I'm sure you knew that." He shrugs his shoulders and tilts his head back toward the load of work he carries.

"May I help you, Gennadius?" I ask, holding open my arms to receive half of the skins. He stops walking and takes a good look at me, this time to discern not my identity, but my intentions.

"Are you trying to get work from me, girl?" he asks.

"Yes, sir. I know tanning is not a woman's trade, but it's the only one I know. I can show you."

"Well...the smell of urine and animal brains hasn't turned you back yet..." he says, looking to the solitary house ahead, half a mile removed from the last home lining the broad road behind us. "In fact," he adds with a sniff. "I think I smell a bit of the trade on *you!*"

I decide not to explain his shrewd observation lest that lead to demands for more information than necessary, so I take the skins from his right shoulder to prove my stomach for them. The tanner smiles in amusement, and at his silent gesture of acceptance, I am surprised to find that I am, in fact, tremendously grateful for it.

⚶

Gennadius leads us around his tiny home to an even smaller tannery, which isn't nearly far enough from the household to keep their noses safe from the fetid fumes. I suppose they, like my family and me, have grown accustomed to the indecent aroma of animal excrement and decaying flesh. The human body has wondrous ways of adapting to cruel conditions; staying upright without vomiting in the midst of this repugnant hovel is no exception.

Inside the tannery sits sleeping a diminutive woman of full, raven hair interwoven with subtle strands of white. The largest pieces of colorless hair frame a face so brown and worn that it resembles the leather her trade produces. Before her feet are two large circular vats, one filled with water and new skins to be softened, the other waiting for our latest delivery.

Gennadius nods toward the empty vat and proceeds to submerge his skins into them. I do the same, as quietly as I can as not to disturb the mistress who looks as though she could sleep until summer.

"Aspasia, wake up, my sweet!" Gennadius shouts. "We have a guest!" His wife slowly opens one eye, not at all startled by our intrusion. My family and I always slept like babies; surrounded by the stench of death, the thought of thieves never crossed our minds.

Gennadius walks over to his wife, takes her by the hand, and helps her to her feet.

"Aspasia, this young lady is a tanner's daughter. Her name is – "

"I know who this girl is. I told you she would be coming, Gennadius," the woman interrupts with a honey-smooth voice that seems to sing. Then she turns to me. "Carya told me you were coming." She begins walking toward me with the glad smile of a grandmother who has known me all of my life.

"Carya?" The question leaps out of me like a lamb from a thicket. Why is that nymph chasing me?

"That is, of course, if you're the girl with the jasper stone..." she says, her voice sliding down along with her gaze, which fixes itself on my girdle.

Unsure if the old woman is a prophetess, a witch, or truly the friend of my childhood comforter, I decide it's best to say nothing and leave before she reads my thoughts...learns about my power. I meet Gennadius's eyes, and with a simple nod try to convey the overwhelming thankfulness I feel for the unearned trust and the warmth of home, however brief, that he gave to me.

As I turn for the door, I feel a gentle hand on my back and am reminded of Acheron's whip.

"The maiden told me your wounds may still need tending to," Aspasia says.

"I have to go," is my stern reply. "My parents taught me better than to keep company with a sorceress. I must say, it's very clever of you to concoct your potions and cast your spells out here. I'm sure the stench turns everyone else away."

"Gennadius, bring some ginger, cinnamon, and calendula." The words hardly escape Aspasia's mouth before her husband leaves us for the healing herbs. "Iris. Look at me, child." I turn around and look into her large jade eyes, surrounded by deep lines of inviting laughter. An enchantress's eyes would be empty of joy and without color; hers are full of both. "You mustn't go. The reward is great for a fugitive's captor," she says.

"And how am I to be sure *you* aren't out for that reward?" I ask with heightening suspicion. I will not be bewitched by this Siren's song. "How can I know that you aren't a Pythonian witch who has learned of me from some plume of smoke or pool of water under a full moon?" Aspasia's smile fades.

"I am no witch. May no one ever think me so, Duna," she implores, looking up through the ceiling toward her god. She lowers her eyes back to mine and takes my hand. "You have good reason to believe that I am untrustworthy, I know. But you must believe...not everyone is your enemy."

I hear the door open behind us followed by the slow footsteps of Gennadius. As if sensing the tension in the room, he lightly kisses his wife's temple and places in her free hand a leather pouch that smells wonderfully of spices. Then he slips a golden calendula flower behind her ear and whispers, "Perhaps you should tell the young lady the message." Aspasia nods, taking the flower from her ear. She twirls it carefully in her fingers before drawing it to her nose, breathing in its vibrancy.

"My husband and I are followers of Duna, child. By his providence, he found it right to send his servant Carya to us with a message. A message for you."

"Carya has given me messages herself!" I exclaim. "Why doesn't she deliver this one?" I too look to the ceiling, opening my arms in invitation to my timid nymph.

"Shhhh...Iris..." With merely two words, my blood is cooled and my pulse slowed by Gennadius's dove-like voice. "When I was a boy I knew the adventures of Odysseus and the labors of Jason and Herakles by heart. I knew them so well that my imagination would often lead me through the woods where it created Cyclopses, Calypso's island, the Cretan Bull..." he chuckles as the boyhood scenes parade past his mind's eye. "I was the bravest warrior, the most renowned hero in all of Limén," he grins, playfully placing his right hand over his breast in solemn salute to his youthful fantasized feats.

Aspasia wraps a bare brown arm around his waist and finishes his thoughts. "Carya is not a figment of your imagination, child. You never dreamed her up, never followed her into a forest planted and watered by Alpha myths and legends. She is as real as we are. And Duna wants you to know it!" She points at me with the calendula's rich green stem and waits for my response.

I pull the jasper stone out of my pouch and cup it in my hands. Closing my eyes, my thoughts travel back to the darkness of last night and the swirling chaos of my dreams; then, bleeding out from those, the nauseous, unfading images of Jasper's body burning on the pyre and Niobe's glassy eyes staring back at me from Acheron's mosaic river.

Do I want truly want vengeance? The question arises not from my brain, but from somewhere deep inside me, calling out like a lost voice echoing against the cold black walls of an unexplored cave. Despite my upbringing, and my inherent regard for life's sanctity and Eusebian honor, I know my answer.

Yes, yes, I want to kill Acheron! I answer back to that unidentifiable echo ascending from my soul. And that is all I must know. That is the first step I must take toward avenging my brother, Niobe, and all the others Acheron has slain.

"I will listen to the nymph's message," I say, opening my eyes to the modest gleam of a sun ray blessing the tannery with ironic sweetness. Aspasia smiles, takes Gennadius's hand, then softly pushes the flower behind my ear and cups my chin in her wrinkled palm.

"Jasper red as blood, healing flower orange as fire,
Your desert journey shall be paved with stones of black desire.
The one you left on the Limén shore was sent to spare you from the knife;
Near the amber scrolls it shall be your turn to speak up for his life."

CHAPTER EIGHT
AMBER

The calendula flower, cheerful as a springtime blossom can be, falls from my ear and drops to the floor. I follow after it, sinking to my knees as the *thump-thump! thump-thump!* of my heart intensifies. I think back to the beautiful blue barn swallow whose wing I fractured as a senseless girl, how I led Jasper to the bridge so he could bandage her and scooped her out of the nest; I felt her fragile heart pound at so furious a pace, I thought she would die from panic. "Shhhhh....shhhhh...I'm only trying to help you," I cooed.

But she never settled down. Not until the bandage was removed, the cage unlatched, and she was free to fly again. Now here I sit, a frightened bird who, even in benevolent hands, cannot quiet itself to be succored.

I smell the cinnamon and ginger as Aspasia makes her way to my side. She sets the leather pouch on the floor and pulls it apart with her bony, branch-like fingers.

"I will put supper on the table," Gennadius says, then respectfully exits so that my back may be exposed to absorb Aspasia's medicine.

"I – I don't think I have much of an appetite," I say, my head aching with a flood of fears, of frustration, certainly, but more than that, of awe. I quake at the indisputable evidence of an all-knowing god, reigning high above the Moonbow, who, for reasons confounding and unknowable, has chosen to speak to *me*, an orphan, a runaway, a huntress tolerating this world just long enough so that one last kill can be made.

⟞⟝

My lacerations freshly covered with Aspasia's salve, I sit comfortably at the tanner's table before a meager bowl of porridge and a disproportionate mound of almonds and walnuts.

I stir the piping hot porridge with a seashell spoon as Aspasia pushes into my elbow a miniature jar of cinnamon. "Thank you..." I say, unsure of its use.

"You put that on your porridge, Iris. It's better that way," Gennadius says, happily sprinkling the spice into his own steaming bowl.

"It's good for your wounds," chimes Aspasia. "And eat the nuts, Iris. They will help you sleep."

"She's right," says Gennadius. "I nibble on a handful every night and scarcely ever hear the noise outside."

"What noise?" I ask, munching on an almond. "There's nothing around. I bet I could hear a pin drop out here."

"The Soukinoi," says Aspasia. "You haven't heard of them?" I shake my head as the alluring scent of cinnamon begins to arouse my appetite. "Oh... well, you may not have heard their name, but you know who they are."

"I've been a slave for three years, my lady. Kept behind walls, only released long enough to fetch water and buy bread."

"Carya revealed to me that you met them at the Okeanos River a few nights ago," says Aspasia, pouring water into my cup.

"'Met' is hardly the right word," I say. "I was captured by a Giant and nearly stabbed to death by a band of outlaws! I suppose Carya left that part out." Gennadius snorts, trying to restrain his laughter. Aspasia calmly takes a sip of water.

"You've been through more than we could possibly comprehend," she says. "I know that good and well. I don't know why Duna has chosen us to take you in, give you his message, feed and shelter you for who knows how long. But he has."

"Did Carya tell you anything else about me?" I ask, wondering if she knows that I'm an Asher.

"Only what her message said. That you're headed to Ēlektōr." Aspasia draws a deep breath through her nostrils, and as she releases it, pulls something from her lap with a clasped hand. She reaches over the table and places in its center a golden, oval-shaped gemstone the size of a dried apricot.

"What is that?" I ask.

"Amber," she replies. "It's where the Soukinoi derived their name...from the Alpha legend. Ēlektōr is their fortress in the desert."

The myth of Helios and his son Phaeton is a popular Alpha dirge. I often began to weep as I passed by the sound of it being played on the kithara at Alpha funerals; the lamenting melody accompanied by woeful - and yet harmonious - sobs made me mourn for a deceased soul I never knew. I have always marveled at the power music has over the human spirit, at its ability to turn time on its head and with one song send captivated minds back to hours of insufferable sorrow... and with the next, to evanescent moments of unbridled ecstasy in which all the world seems to glisten, basking in a mist of sublime satisfaction.

I hum the tune quietly and listen to my memories sing the words:

"Phaeton, boy born shining,
Child thirsting to climb the sky.
Phaeton, boy born pining,
Your ambition made you fly.
Upon the chariot of the sun you filled history with your name,
For you lost control of the fiery steeds and died in scorching flame."

"Yes, you know 'Helios's Lament' quite well, child," Aspasia says, smiling softly as I murmur the last words aloud: *"And died in scorching flame."* Tears rise quickly from the bottomless cistern of my soul as I think of Jasper, my innocent brother, who also died in scorching flame...

"Do you know the rest of the story?" Gennadius asks. I wipe my eyes, shake my head, and blow on a hot spoonful of porridge to distract myself from my emotions. "Dear, why don't you explain?" Aspasia takes a breath, then draws the piece of amber back into her hands and peers into it as though it were a sacred artifact, a prize awarded by Helios the Sun God himself.

"The legend goes that after Phaeton's death, his mother and sisters searched the world over for his tomb," Aspasia begins, stroking the stone like a sleeping cat. "And when they found it, they stood around it and wept. For four months they wept.

"At the end of their mourning, they tried to leave, but could not take a step. They were as trees, rooted to the earth, and poplar trees they became, hardening fast with bark from head to foot." Aspasia pauses and holds up the amber for me to see. "*This* is what their tears became. Solid amber."

I reach for the amber, then look to Aspasia for permission to handle it. She nods. As I examine the fossil, I imagine that it truly is a remnant of the goddesses' tears, translucent, tangible symbols of age-old human suffering...

And then I remember that the goddesses were not human at all, *if* they even existed. What I hold in my hand is nothing more than resin, an oozing secretion that was fortunate enough to avoid the disintegrating effects of sun and rain.

"A tragic story," I say, returning the stone to Aspasia. "But Phaeton and his weeping trees are a made-up Alpha tale. What have they to do with the Soukinoi you spoke of?"

"Soukinoi is the ancient word for amber," Gennadius says, with the didactic air of a schoolmaster. He rubs his gray, bearded chin, contemplating what to say next. But instead of speaking, he reaches over and takes his wife's hand.

"Our son was one of them," Aspasia says, squeezing Gennadius's fingers and the amber stone simultaneously. "He brought the stone to us the night he told us he was leaving. He said –" She takes a deep brave breath, releases her husband's hand, and wipes her eyes before proceeding. "He said the Soukinoi had stolen the scrolls of the Eusebian Oracles at the Temple in Eirene...for *safe keeping,* he'd said. The most sacred passages, all the prophecies, are sealed in – "

"Inside the amber," I answer. "So they call themselves Soukinoi after the scrolls?"

"Yes," Aspasia nods. "They say the Oracles and we, the followers of the Hodos, have wrongly judged the prophecies and are unfit to protect them from Eusebian delinquents or Alpha thieves."

My brother was among the Hodos, that is, *the Way,* a Eusebian sect birthed seven years ago after the report of Python's defeat by Phos in the Great Sea spread like a fever through the countryside and city streets, imbuing pedantic old philosophers and cynical young heathens with faith in their forgotten god.

Jasper told me that Phos' sacrificial death would liberate us from the evil of Python and transform all of Petros into a new world, an indestructible, unconquerable, peaceful and eternal elysium called Adamas... But most Eusebians, and I am one of them, are not blind. We still see the baleful works of Python rippling out of the Great Sea like the venom-tipped tentacles from a monstrous squid. We have heard the howling of Harpies at the midnight hour, the screeching of a sphinx on starless nights, and see the hoof-shaped scars of Centaurs imprinted on the hands and feet of Eusebian children.

If Phos was victorious, why do the innocent still suffer?

"Our son joined the Soukinoi because he believed in their cause; he died fighting for it," says Gennadius. "Our friends saw his body strapped to the back of an Alpha horse parading through the streets of Eirene."

Aspasia begins to weep.

"He was just a boy," her voice cracks. "A boy who thought himself an Achaean bound for the shores of Troy. He had a hero's heart, our son."

"What *is* the Soukinoi cause?" I ask.

"They are planning to wage war against the Alphas. At least, that is what they claim," says Aspasia. "They recruit young Eusebians like the outlaws you met at the Okeanos. And like you..." Aspasia and Gennadius both look at me wistfully, sadness burning beneath their eyes, and I wonder if their minds have transformed me into a vision of their son.

"I believe your son was a hero, Gennadius," I say. "I'm sorry he's not here to join us tonight at your table. And, forgive me, but I think the Soukinoi are brave for standing against the Alphas."

"Brave men must also be wise men," Gennadius replies. "The Soukinoi terrorize for the thrill of it. They are stabbing people in the streets just for repairing Alpha sandals or selling them bread. "It is madness." He strikes his fist on the table and furrows his brow, just as my father did when addressing matters he considered idiotic, reprehensible, or unjust. "Madness," he repeats.

"Iris, you were nearly murdered because you were enslaved by an Alpha. Don't you see? They don't do this out of honor, but hatred!" Aspasia says.

"It isn't true," I whisper.

"What did you say? I am an old man, girl," Gennadius says, using a ragged voice as he cups his hand over an ear.

"I said it isn't true," I say louder. "I met a Soukinos who saved my life...twice. The first time at the Okeanos and then again on the ship that brought me here."

"Yes. Tycho," Aspasia says.

My heart skips a beat, and I can barely utter, "How do you know him?"

"Everyone in Limn knows of him. He was once a Pythonian, and then, Duna knows why, chose to join the Soukinoi. He became the outlaws' most notorious cut-throat. Praise Duna that he isn't any longer," Gennadius says. "He was responsible for the slaughter of dozens of Eusebians."

"He *still* is an outlaw," I object. "He was at the river just two nights ago, when he saved my life."

Gennadius and Aspasia exchange glances, and then linger in silence, as if waiting for me to break it.

"What is it?" I demand.

"Iris, that night was Tycho's last as a Soukinos," Aspasia says. "She didn't tell him why, but Carya asked him to endure one final mission. And now, wherever he is, he knows the reason – to rescue *you*."

"I could have rescued myself. I have..." I pause, silently debating whether to tell them about the doma.

The amber stone begins to glow, and tingling chills begin to cover my arms as I am reminded of Carya's words to Aspasia. I remember my imminent journey to the Soukinoi and their "amber walls"...to Tycho and his imperiled life. And I am warmed by the thought that as long as these prophecies ultimately lead me to the cesspool where I will scatter Acheron's ashes, then I will embrace each one with an Oracle's adoration.

Without warning, the warmth inside me grows feverish. The chills on my arms disappear in an instant and sweat glistens in their place. I open my hands just slightly to see them glowing yellow like the amber stone.

"Are you all right, child?" Gennadius asks. "She looks ill, dear," he says, placing a hand on Aspasia's arm. "Maybe it's the porridge..."

"I'm...I'm fine," I lie. "I just need to sleep, I think. You've been very kind to me. I'll see you in the morning." I lie again. I have no intention of staying here through the night. I am determined to make it to the Soukinoi fortress and join others like myself, others who want what I want, who will appreciate what I'm capable of. "Thank you for supper." I slide my chair back and stand, pressing my burning palms into my tunic, hoping they'll burn again when the time is right.

CHAPTER NINE
CENTAUR

Aspasia was wrong. The almonds and walnuts don't help me sleep. I sit on my bed, facing the window and running my fingers along the blade of my Soukinoi dagger. I stare at the rustic weapon, transfixed by it as it flickers, dancing in a silky stream of moonlight pouring through the window. I wonder how many lives it has taken since leaving the blacksmith's hands. I wonder how many lives it will take in mine, or if I will even need it.

Before my imagination can carry me into a crimson-colored nightmare, I hear a loud shout outside the window. *Soukinoi,* I think. The child within me, pitiable wraith that she is, wants to dive into the corner and cower until her brother comes to assuage her fears with strong arms and soft singing. But the avenger in me, less a girl and more a hunter with each passing hour, wants to test the caliber of my courage, to prove whether I am truly ready to join the ranks of the Soukinoi or if I'm still a worthless wanderer, self-deceived by a head full of heroes' tales and a heart of intractable anger.

I fetch my cloak, resolved to either hunt down the source of the shouting voice or venture into the desert, to Ēlektōr, as Carya's prophecy said I would.

I tiptoe through the house, careful not to wake Gennadius and Aspasia, though both of them snore dreadfully beneath a bundle of linen blankets; it is obvious why they're never stirred by the ruckus outside.

I step onto the empty street and turn westward where the young waxing moon hangs low over the quiet homes of Limén. No shouts, no snoring, only misty rain and roaming cats darting in and out of alleyways. I turn around and gasp at the sight of the Moonbow towering untold miles above the mountains. Each of its seven arches seem to pulsate with a life all their own, a vibrant heart beating, silent but strong, within the body of sleeping sky.

"Come and get me you stinking swine!"

The taunting shout of a young girl's voice leads me to the tannery, the stench of which is made more nauseating by the presence of a Pythonian Centaur stalking the premises like a half-starved mutt.

I duck behind a large pot, which thankfully lacks its usual malodorous liquid, and aided by the Moonbow's brilliance, study the miserable beast for whom the folk stories do no justice. In the songs and nursery tales, Centaurs are almost always accurately portrayed as savages and drunkards, but the description of their physical appearance is surprisingly sparse; perhaps the imagination is left to wonder because, if given the facts, young children would never sleep at night.

From his rust-colored hooves to his rubicund face, this half-man, half-horse creature stands over eight feet tall. His shaggy sorrel coat is matted and patchy, a result of the warming weather and an indolent disregard for baths. His shoulders and withers are darkened with perspiration, his heaving flanks washed white with foam, and from the ample girth of his belly, I hear the repulsive gurgling of an appetite that never wanes. Almost camouflage against his body is a leather strap buckled around his midsection with an empty scabbard attached to it; I wonder if a sword is meant for it.

Above the equine shoulders, the Centaur is a man from waist to head – albeit, a man who looks as though he's been cursed with unequaled ugliness by the mischievous goddess, Aite. His chest and arms, though undoubtedly strong, are covered in curly chestnut hair that sticks together in greasy clumps of dried sweat, dirt, and bits of food. His fingernails, uncut and coated with soil, remind me of an eagle's talons. His head is completely shaven and, surprisingly, without bump or blemish...save for the Pythonian tattoo. Positioned behind the Centaur, I can see only the fat black line of the serpent's meandering tail tracing along his spine up onto his scalp.

"Up here!" The girl's voice cries out like a banshee from the roof of the tannery. As I turn my head I hear the Centaur grunt and paw the ground as his attention also shifts to Gennadius's shed.

The front of his face now visible, I see the Centaur's narrow, deep-set eyes and make out the serpent's triangular head and its hissing tongue trailing down the length of his misshapen nose. The creature whinnies wildly, his stallion-like madness now provoked, and takes off galloping around and around the tannery, his tail thrashing harder with every dizzying turn. I wrap myself like a barnacle around the pot and slide around it until I am tightly wedged between it and the tannery's brick wall and can see nothing but an unending line of jagged mountain peaks barring the way to wilderness.

I hear the clamorous sound of the Centaur's hooves landing on the thatched roof above my head and out of view. He snorts three times, then speaks in a guttural voice and with a crude, unfamiliar accent that scrapes at my ears.

"A clever rat, you are," he says. "You've done this many times before, haven't you. Stealing Centaur swords has become a little game, has it?"

"My favorite game in the world, right after ostrakinda," the girl replies coolly.

Ostrakinda... I had forgotten that game and how much I loved to insist to my brother and his friends that I be allowed to play it with them.

"You're too little, Iris. You'll be smashed like a bug," Jasper would say.

"I'd rather be smashed like a bug than pent up like a bird inside with mother dicing onions," I'd pout.

I can see Jasper now, sighing and then smiling at my stubbornness as he took from his tunic the oyster shell for which the game was named. "Then you're on my team. You stay with me."

I smile now remembering how elated I became at the sound of those words. I would take my big brother's hand and join his side as teams were chosen, one called "Night" and the other "Day." One side of the shell was smeared black to represent Night's team, while the stainless side symbolized Day's.

My brother would toss the shell into the air, and the team whose color struck the ground faceup took off in pursuit of the other. Captors, when tagged, were made Centaurs who then carried the victors on their backs as they chased down the remaining foot soldiers. My favorite part was towering above the rest of our playmates, I latched onto Jasper's back, he upon the back of his make-believe Centaur shouting "Turn right! Over there! Behind that Juniper!"

"You and your little rodent friends are collecting our weapons for your pathetic revolt, are you?" the Centaur huffs, his voice growing louder as his hooves advance across the roof.

"Do you know what ostrakinda is, half-breed?"

"A game. You just said that. Do you think I am a moron?!" the beast yells.

"Well if it is all right with you, I would like to play it with you now!"

I now regret having taken this seat among what has proven a most unlikely theater; it's doubtful the comedy presently unfolding will end with laughter and applause. I consider how I might sneak away, hoping that a role has not been written for me. I decide to stay put, fearing that a sudden move might mark my accidental entrance onto the bizarre moonlit stage spread out above me.

"Here!" the girl continues. A few seconds pass before I hear the sound of an object hitting the roof with a soft thud; I know it is an oyster shell. "Night! That means you're it, half-breed! Come and get me!"

I hear the Centaur dig his fore hooves into the roof so hard I fear it might collapse beneath his fury. Carefree as a foal, the girl whinnies, launches the sword from the roof, then springs off of it herself, landing beside it, just three yards from where I hide. As soon as her feet hit the ground, she crumbles onto her knees and cries out in agony.

Where is the family that once comforted her? I think.

The Centaur makes his move. He leaps from the tannery and lands beside her, his pugnacious pest. Savoring each moment before he will surely trample and break every bone in her body, he approaches slowly, and then begins circling her like a corpse ready to be scavenged.

"You won't scamper off so easily this time. Let's see...I've had fish bones, dog bones and wolf bones," the Centaur smacks his lips. "But never have I had a Eusebian girl's bones in my soup. I hope they don't make me ill the way your face does." The girl tries to stand but falls helplessly and begins to crawl toward a non-existent refuge somewhere in the distance.

I feel the hair on the back of my neck bristling and my fingers tightening around my dagger. It might be time for me to intervene and try my hand at playing the *apò mēkhanḗs theós* – drama's grand "god from the machine" who is lowered to the stage by a crane with the task of resolving the mortals' conflicts.

"I'll just need that sword of mine before I can cook my supper..." boasts the beast, who then ducks his head and begins his charge.

"No! Please!" cries the girl, as loudly and as desperately as she can. To my surprise, the Centaur stops, and I begin to move, inching out of the shadows so the light can reveal how fearless, or how hopeless, I really am. I stare down at my hands, willing a fire to catch inside them, but they insist on remaining damp and dark in the rain.

"What is it - you have a few last words you'd like to say to the Moonbow over there?" the Centaur says.

"It isn't worth it. I'm hurt, and I can barely lift your sword anyway," the girl says, turning onto her back and throwing the sword a few scant inches in the sand, separating her wounded body from hell-shod hooves.

"Mighty Soukina...You should have killed me when you had the chance. That will cost you."

As the Centaur steps toward her, I shut my eyes and fling my dagger as hard and as fast as I can toward his lower half. I hear a terrible yelp and open my eyes to see the Centaur fall onto his haunches with my blade protruding from them like a pin in a pomegranate, and I wonder how he felt it at all.

"Pssssst!" I hiss. The girl looks at me, jumps to her feet, and with two arms hurls the heavy sword in my direction. *A clever girl indeed...*

Next, the sprite sprints to the blade stuck in the Centaur's backside and yanks it out, eliciting another earsplitting wail from the beast. The girl runs to my side, her windblown yellow hair and peach, cherubic cheeks masking her devilish bent.

"What took you so long?" she asks, jabbing me in the ribs with the butt of my knife.

With no time for questions, I lift the sword with two hands, point it at the Centaur, and remind myself that this isn't a game. The losers don't shake hands with the winners, then wash up and return home for dinner.

"I can wield this sword just fine, Centaur," I say. He looks at me suspiciously and limps toward me. "I didn't have to miss with the knife. I very easily could have sent it flying into the base of your skull, right through that serpent's tail," I lie.

"And why did you show such *mercy*, might I ask?" snarls the beast, mockery replacing the hunger on his lips.

"Because you have something I want," I say. "And I am willing to spare your life for it."

"And what do I have that you could possibly need," questions the Centaur.

"Four legs. I need them to get me to the Soukinoi fortress. Then I will let you go."

She elbows my side and whispers, "I'm going with you."

"You should go home and stop playing Soldier," I reply, yanking my knife from her hand.

"Ēlektōr *is* my home," says the girl. "And I know how to get there." I squint at her skeptically and tap my dagger against my thigh. "Fine," says the girl, reading my uncertainty. "If you wish to be stranded out in the middle of the desert with a Centaur who will likely eat you alive when he gets hungry in a few hours, be my guest!" The girl curtsies indignantly and turns to walk away.

"Wait!" I call out after her. She turns back to me, hands on her hips. "You can come. But I'm not responsible for looking after you."

"I look after myself," she yips.

"I can respect that," I smile. "I do, too."

The Centaur doesn't say a word. He paws his hoof into the ground.

I lift my dagger to my face, poised to throw. "Go ahead. Try running. I can tell you want to." The Centaur tosses his head and neighs bitterly at the Moonbow as it shines upon his misfortune.

With the sword's tip I draw a semicircle in the sand. During my years as Acheron's slave, I learned that Centaurs give their word by finishing the circle offered them. The penalty for dishonoring the oath is abandonment by his herd – his family.

"Hurry up, half-breed! You've heard her terms!" shouts the girl.

"I have already broken the Centaurian Oath once," says the Centaur, in a purely human voice. "That's why I am here chasing down petty thieves, schoolgirl thieves at that."

"In that case, Centaur, you can be sure the punishment will be far more severe should you break the oath a second time," I say.

The Centaur shakes his head, swats the rain with his tail, then lowers himself onto his front knees and leans forward. "I doubt it can get much worse," he says. "I have disgraced my entire kind by bowing down to the likes of you." And with that, he stretches over the semicircle and completes it with an uncontrollable grimace.

CHAPTER TEN
OASIS

You'd better start explaining yourself before I change my mind and take my chances in the desert without you," I whisper to the girl as we ride atop the Centaur, Limén fading behind us, a mirage glimmering in the awakening haze of desert heat.

"You wouldn't return to the old man if you knew what was good for you," she replies, eyes straight ahead, tone as flat as the barren terrain before us.

"And what does that mean?"

"You told Lysander and the other Soukinoi that you would kill Acheron. Did you?"

"How do you know about that," I demand.

"I told you already – I'm one of them. And I was there."

"So you know..."

"About your doma? Of course I do."

"How did you find me? Do you have a doma for following a person's scent? Or maybe you're part canine?"

The girl snickers like a child. "No! But I have something better." She turns to me and lowers her head as if to whisper. "A *Gryphon!*" She shrieks the word as loud as she can and crazily bats her arms, causing the Centaur to trot ahead nervously and my anxious blood to warm.

"Careful. You don't want to upset me," I say, placing her hand on my pulsing forearm. Her eyes and smile widen with curiosity. "And Gryphons don't exist," I add.

"You'll see. She was released to track you, and found you at Ourania. Then she brought me to Limén to hunt you down."

"You rode a Gryphon here?" I laugh at such a ridiculous-sounding question.

"I didn't swim or fly here myself."

"If the Gryphon is real, why didn't it just kill me back at the port?"

"She's a secret," the girl whispers. "We don't want the whole world knowing she's not just a myth. Anyway, stop changing the subject. Acheron is still alive. It was my job to kill you back there."

I think of Gennadius and Aspasia. They probably woke up just minutes ago and walked into my room to invite me for breakfast, only to find my bed disheveled and empty. I can see Aspasia's green eyes widening with worry and welling with tears, and Gennadius's old callused hand clenching hers before leaving to brew for her a consoling cup of tea.

"Incredible...Your job to kill me..." I laugh, my concern for my forsaken hosts diminishing in the wake of this brazen child's audacity. "If it had not been for me, you would be inside this Centaur's belly instead of on top of it."

The girl and I begin to bounce up and down as the Centaur chortles.

"Stop it!" I demand, kicking his sides. He whinnies and trots a few yards until his laughter subsides.

"My ankles were never broken. Did you fail to notice?" the girl says, lifting her legs and pointing her toes as she turns her feet left and right for me to see. "I knew you were following us. I could see you from the roof. So I decided to test you."

"You risked your life just to see if I would save you?" I ask.

The girl slips her hand into a large pouch fastened to her girdle and reveals from it the end of a dagger's sheath. She pats it proudly. "I was ready to kill him if I needed to. Then you," she grins.

I slide back a few inches, trying in vain to distance myself from this cunning child-warrior who has made me into a fool. I feel the Centaur laughing again, but I don't stop him this time. I deserve every bit of his glee-laced ridicule.

"Don't be so upset. You have nothing to worry about now, Iris. You're one of us," the girl assures me. "Why didn't you kill him?" she asks, her tone more somber now. "You had the perfect chance…"

"It wasn't perfect!" I protest. "He had just strangled his favorite slave and left her body lying in the andron like a pile of soiled laundry." The bolts of heat shoot through me. Hot yellow halos glow around my palms. "He'd always been suspicious of us because we are Eusebians. She set him off. And I was next on his list."

With that, the halos break apart, giving way to searing red flames. The Centaur freezes, the girl ducks, flattening herself over his shoulders, and I scream, extending my hands toward the mountains. The spheres of fire, bigger than before, crisscross each other in midair and emblazon the sky with twin trails of blinding light.

"Impressive!" snorts the Centaur.

"And that didn't happen when I tried to destroy Acheron's house," I confess, watching the fireball dissipate in the distance.

"You could have killed him with your dagger," the girl counters. "If you want to be a Soukina, you'll have to learn the value of sacrifice," the girl says with the sober conviction of a soldier. I have no doubt but that the lofty line is a Soukinoi dictum instilled in her the day she ran away from home and joined the desert rebels.

"You can't be older than twelve. – "

"I'm fourteen!" she snaps.

"You're still a child, far too young to be stealing Pythonian swords and assassinating slaves like me."

"I haven't got a choice, do I?!" I feel heat radiate from her body as she elevates her voice in outrage. "Children like me must fight the Alphas because older, *wiser* Eusebians like you are too afraid!"

The girl's words simultaneously sting and sadden me. I am pained by the reality that for the past seven years, I have been a coward, a compliant slave to the man who murdered my brother to assuage his injured ego. But I am also grieved as what little sympathy I have left lurches in my heart for the teenaged outlaw sitting in front of me, a girl who likely will not live to see her next birthday.

⊰ↄ/ↄ/ↄ⊱

Hardly any more words are spoken for the duration of our journey. The few that are concern the single oasis the girl promised we would reach soon enough, "after we forget what water tastes like."

When the Centaur sees it, he starts to lope as swiftly as his tired muscles will allow and sends me sliding off his hindquarters onto the hot sand where I sit for some time while my cohorts cackle until their dry throats give out and they take off into the water.

"You tried to kill each other a few hours ago, and now you frolic together like Poseidon's sea nymphs?!" I yell after them, but they pretend not to hear as they splash and swim from shore to shore, getting their fill of the refreshing pool.

As I walk toward the water, I see on the other side what I think first to be a mirage, but the more I blink and the harder I squint, the more distinct it becomes – an Alpha army on horseback, headed straight for us.

My survival instincts overpowering the impulse to run, I throw aside the sword, untie my sandals, and dive into the water which I then begin to lap rapaciously into my mouth. When common sense returns, I climb out, wring my chiton free of as much moisture as I can, and look up to see the Centaur bounding out of the water, clearly alarmed by the wall of riders on the horizon.

"Where are you going?" the girl calls after us, floating like a sun-soaked cloud on the surface of the water. I point toward the coming cavalry. She swims to shallower water, stands up, and beams at the horde as if it were a festival parade passing through.

"Let's get out of here! If those are Pythonian, I'll be dead and you'll be made slaves or left stranded here!" shouts the Centaur.

"It's Titus!"the girl proclaims and then rushes onto dry land and stands waving her arms beneath one of seven palm trees that form a green ring of life around the oasis.

"Titus is the Soukinoi general," the Centaur says to me. "If you grant that the rebel rats have an army..." he smirks.

I point the sword at the ground in front of the Centaur. "Kneel," I say. Rolling his eyes, the Centaur obeys.

"What now. Are we going to run to meet them, your new family?" he asks. I slap the back of his arm, weary of his sarcasm. "I fear to go too fast. You might fall off again."

"Stop it, Centaur! I don't know 'what now,' but you're in this with me. That was the deal," I say, swinging onto his back.

"The deal was that I would get you to the fortress," he corrects me. I look out at the fast-moving army, the walls of wilderness around us, and realize that he's absolutely right. He could run back to Limén, save his own neck, and I wouldn't be around to tell his Centaur kinsmen that he'd betrayed me. "But I'm not that fast," he adds. "I think I'll take my chances."

The Centaur takes me to the girl, and there we stand in silence, waiting expectantly for the arrival of a general who may waste no time demanding our execution.

⁃⁃⁃❰◦/◦/◦❱⁃⁃⁃

"Good afternoon, princess. I'm sure glad to see you. You know how your brother worries." The Soukinoi general dismounts a majestic gray mare dotted red with freckles. Titus is well over six feet tall, at least fifty years old with tan, weathered skin, high broad cheek bones, and the militant bearing of a man who is neither amused nor surprised by anything. He takes the reins and leads the horse to the girl who throws her arms around its neck. "You should have taken her with you."

The girl releases her horse. "I would not have risked her being stolen and sold to some Alpha Guardian. Not in a million years!" She kisses the mare's muzzle. "I apologize for causing my brother concern. But I was delayed by a Centaur..."

Titus eyes the Centaur and walks closer toward him. "Well now we know where that heinous odor is coming from," Titus says, sending a wave of laughter rippling along the first line of roughly forty soldiers. "Alexa, I don't know you to be so merciful. Pray tell, what did he do to fall into your good graces?"

"He did nothing. The *slave* decided to negotiate with him," says the girl, pointing an accusatory finger at me as though I had committed some dastardly crime. Titus spins in the sand to face me.

"It only makes sense," says the general, looking at me with a stiff, inscrutable countenance. "She was negotiated with at Okeanos. As were some of the most courageous of all Soukinoi warriors," he continues, almost at a whisper.

He walks over to me and stands within inches of my face. I look up and find copper-colored eyes that are not filled with hostility as Lysander's were, nor vainglory like the girl's. "I hope you are ready for what lies ahead of you, Iris," he whispers.

CHAPTER ELEVEN
ĒLEKTŌR

It is the longest, blackest night I've ever endured. So hushed is the desert and so distant the stars that I put my hand before my face and clap three times to make sure I have not gone deaf and blind with lunacy. The Centaur on whom I ride begins to trot; evidently, he is easily spooked.

"Don't get antsy now. Get some sleep and we'll be there before you wake up," I hear a soldier say. I see his silhouette turned toward us, and I nod my head.

"Yes, sir," I reply. And at the mention of sleep my head becomes heavy as a millstone. I decide not to inform the Centaur that I'll be napping, and the second I let my chin drop to my chest, my family steps into my dreams...

The four of us sit on the windswept cliffs overlooking the Great Sea, not far from our tannery in Eirene. My father, his back to the water, reclines on a limestone rock while Jasper, my mother and I sit facing him on a woolen, sandy brown blanket littered with crumbs from our midday meal.

My parents are young and ravishing in the summer sun. My father's beard is thick and black, my mother's fair face the envy of Aphrodite. My brother and I are the happiest of children, our skinned elbows and bruised knees souvenirs from our many treks up and down this mountain, sometimes to buy salt or find dung for our father's work, but mostly we run where our imaginations lead us – to the enchanted isle of Circe, the harrowing maze of Theseus and the Minotaur, the wooden horse of Troy, the lair of snake-haired Medusa, and when a fishing boat is left unattended, the god-built *Argo* of Jason.

My father places a hand over his brow to shield his eyes from the sun, and then winks at me.

"Iris, are you ready to begin?" he asks.

I nod my head excitedly and then rummage through a basket until I find it – a cork mask my father carved for me after accompanying Jasper and me to our very first play not long ago. From the first act to the fifth, all I could talk about were those masks, some contorted in ghoulish, unnatural expressions, others pristine, placid, and painted with pastels. Some featured pointed ears and red satyrs' horns curving backward, others were topped with gilded laurels. But all transformed the amphitheater into a fairyland rife with Cyclopses, sea monsters, warriors and witches. I was hypnotized by the masks and insisted to my father that I must have one so I too could become dauntless, dazzling, colorful, crafty, simply by donning a thespian's mask.

The mask I hold in my hands has not been painted yet, nor does it have horns or a chaplet with which to adorn my head. It is ordinary, nondescript, without frills or emotion, "suited for any adventure of the stage," my father had said.

I place it on my head and go to him, eager to enact whichever drama or comedy he orates. But rather than standing to take his place as the leading *hypokrites* – "the one who interprets" – he smiles warmly and whispers, "It is your turn to perform."

I shake my head. "No, papa, I don't know the story! I don't know my lines!" I say vehemently. My father places a hand on my shoulder.

"I know, my dear. You must improvise."

Before I can argue further, the mazarine sky turns menacing over the ocean, churning ferociously in smoky whorls of black and gray. As if breaking through a dam, a deluge of rain is released, bringing with it forceful winds that push me onto the gravel-laden ground.

"Stay here, on the rock," my father says calmly, pulling me up. He stands and makes his way to Jasper and my mother who are hastily packing up our perfect picnic scene.

"Wait! Wait for me!" I cry out, but my voice is swallowed by the squall's unforgiving gusts. I try to remove the mask, but no matter how hard I twist and pull and pry, it doesn't budge. I look up toward my family and see them leaving, each running with a basket over their heads toward home.

"Don't leave me!" I yell, vocal chords straining to send the words flying on the wings of the wind. But the wind is pitiless, my voice weak, and though I can't feel the warmth of my tears through the rain or hear the sound of my cries through the storm, I know that I am weeping harder than I ever have. In fact, to this point in my life, I have never known the kind of soul-deep suffering that can fill the body, from breath to bone, with the bitter cold of the moon's dark face...

My family now hidden somewhere beneath the canopy of fir trees covering the mountain, my gaze rises to the only face left before me – that of the moon's, smiling boldly into nature's belligerence and the eyes of a deserted child. Then, before this child's eyes, the moon's surface begins to undulate, morphing into a winter-white pond quickened by the bashful light of spring.

I stare into it, mesmerized by the rise and fall of these impossible lunar waves, and watch as the waters recede, rolling away into blackness until nothing remains but a disk of smooth obsidian...a mirror...

The wind quiets, the rain softens, and I abandon the rock, anxious to see what the moon is reflecting, to see if it will reveal my family rushing back for me now that the storm has ceased.

But what I see shining inside the iridescent orb is my own masked face! I see my hands slapping at it, tugging desperately to tear it away and throw it into the ocean, but as I pull, the mask begins to take on the color of my flesh. *It's coming off! It's coming off!* I think. But as I stand and watch, waiting for the mask to liquefy and fall like rain onto my feet, I am sickened by the image the moon is unveiling.

"No!" I shout. "Go away! Stop it!" But the face doesn't stop; it mimics my every syllable. It is my face, the wicked face of Acheron.

I jump out of the dream with an audible gasp, startling the Centaur who curses under his breath.

"You enjoy your sleep, your highness?" he asks facetiously.

I pat my face with my hands, comb my fingers through my hair, then pull out the jasper stone and press it to my lips.

"Centaur, I never thought I'd be so happy to see you," I say. And I mean it. Before that dream, never would I have fathomed that one day I could feel relieved to be sitting atop a begrimed and barbaric half-breed while roaming through an utter wasteland in between ranks of armed rebels. But life often proves we don't know ourselves as well as we'd supposed; what we couldn't possibly conceive of at daybreak can be our reality by dusk.

"Are you happy to see *this*?" says the Centaur, his hairy finger pointing ahead.

The solider who spoke to me last night was right. While I slept, the Centaur had carried me all the way to the Soukinoi fortress – at least, I assume it is their fortress because it is the only structure as far as the eye can see. It doesn't look much like a fortress at all, but rather appears to be the dilapidated ruins of an Alpha temple.

Six massive limestone columns rise elegantly to a mildly pitched wooden roof. The old temple's façade is made of marble and features what surely was once a spectacular frieze of gods and heroes engaged in war, which, as the esteemed Alpha thinkers said long ago, has "always existed by nature," and is "king of all of us." I'm sure it was the sculptor's intention to portray not only the gore and glory of war, but its inextricable presence in the ages, one that not even the greatest of peacemakers or wisest of sages will ever be able to banish. At the mercy of the Eusebian revolutionaries, however, the tableau is degraded to a canvas, its supernal faces marred by the hate-filled Soukinoi with garish colors of paint.

At Titus's command, the soldiers break formation. Some dismount and talk amongst themselves, others ride freely past the temple, whooping wildly until they are out of sight, lost behind a cloud of sand and a blinding sun.

"Welcome to Ēlektōr." I look down to see Alexa holding out her hand. "Your weapon." I hand the sword to her.

"That would be *my* weapon," the Centaur says.

"Half-breed, you own nothing!" Alexa says sharply, raising the sword to his throat.

"Don't hurt yourself, girl," the Centaur laughs.

"Titus!" Alexa calls, lowering the sword and shaking her weakened arms one at a time.

Not a minute later, the general approaches. "Are you all right, princess?" he asks.

"Have this sack of scum put in a cell. He vexes me..." she says, cheeks reddening, jaw tightening.

Titus gives an obedient nod and unsheathes his sword. "Come with me," he orders the Centaur.

"I kept my oath!" the Centaur shouts. "I am free to go!"

"He's right," I say, unable to keep out of it. "We had an agreement. He was to get the girl and me here, and then I would permit him to leave."

"And who do you think you are..." Alexa says, her volatile eyes homing in on me like a hornet. "What makes you think you have the right to *permit* anything?!"

"I gave him my word. As a Eusebian. If that means anything here..."

"It means we don't make deals with Pythonian parasites!" she screams. "It means we know better than to believe a word they say. The second he's back in Limén, he'll tell all his Alpha friends where we are. All it takes is a few left-over ribs or a piglet runt to bribe a Centaur."

"Any fire in those hands of yours?" the Centaur growls at me.

"And to you, *princess,* your word means trick and deceive until you get your way. Sounds Pythonian if you ask- "

"That's enough," Titus stops me. "I didn't come here to moderate moral disputes, but to do as I'm told. Come with me, Centaur."

The Centaur turns his head toward me. "Looks like your ride is over," he says, then kneels for me to climb down. I do so reluctantly.

"You're lucky you're being kept alive, half-breed!" yells Alexa.

"I'm so sorry," I whisper to him. He looks down at the ground and paws at it, this time not out of ire, but uneasiness – he's afraid.

"I bet you've got sweet bones," he says wryly.

"Sweeter than the girl's," I joke.

The Centaur gives a hoarse laugh as he takes his place beside Titus, whose sword is raised, ready to prod its captive to his confinement.

CHAPTER TWELVE
OATH

Before I humiliate myself by shedding a tear for the Centaur, Alexa pulls on my cloak.

"Come on. We're going to meet Diokles," she says.

"Who?" I ask.

"My brother. Our leader."

"The one who ordered you to stalk me...and to *kill* me if you had the chance?" I ask, incredulous.

The girl laughs. "You may want to make a good impression. Don't say too much."

I follow her up the temple steps, past rows of bronze incense burners and through the colonnades, straight to the east-facing door of the cella, opened just enough for the admission of necessary sunlight. She presses her forefinger to her lips.

"Shh!"

I roll my eyes and then fix them on the once-hallowed earth below, where spotless animals had been sacrificed and votive offerings bought and sold by devout Alphas decades – if not centuries – ago, before their leaders decided to disown their gods, relegate them to bedtime fables and theater farces, and govern by their own wits.

Though I don't know which gods of the countryside – the *Theo Nomio*, as the Alphas called them – this temple once honored, I know that they are far from here, perhaps patronizing more pious realms of Petros. Or then again, maybe they truly never did exist at all, except in the minds of the ancient dreamers who sought to answer the riddles of the world, harness the unknown forces hovering above and flowing through it, and with luck, find favor with them.

"Come from the four winds of the earth, O breath.
Breathe into these dead that they may live again."

A raspy, unctuous voice echoes against the walls of the cella, reciting words every Eusebian child memorizes before their mouths can form them.

"So I gave the oracle as you told me.
And breath flew in from the winds and brought life to the dead.
And they all stood up together, a great army of Duna."

This is one of the most famous and most cherished Eusebian prophecies; it foretells the resurrection of the spirit and will of our people, and a promised liberation from those who have oppressed us for so long. It seems that whoever is speaking believes the oracle's fulfillment to be close at hand.

"Let's go!" Alexa whispers.

We walk slowly into the gloomy inner chamber. Strangely, I feel no angst entering the presence of the man who has been expecting a positive report of my death. It seems that any natural, sensible desire to flee has been superseded by my curiosity to meet the one responsible for galvanizing so many of my people, and threatening the lives of many others. But then, even if I did try to run, how far would I make it before Alexa or another of her comrades flung a knife or sword into my back? Probably no farther than the marble effigies of warring heroes carved into the temple pediment. And no matter if they are nothing more than stone renderings of beings sprung from the arcane crevices of men's minds, I still do not wish to die a deserter's death before them.

Alexa shuts the door behind us and motions for me to join her standing still against it. The cella is dark, illuminated only by a few small terracotta oil lamps flickering along the perimeter. At the farthest end of the room is a small niche in the wall, about three feet high and no wider than me. The speaker stands beneath the lamplight and continues to read:

"Then you will know that you are my people, and
That I am Duna, your God.
You will know what I have spoken,
And that I have done it."

The speaker turns so that I can see his profile. If not for his position under the light, he would be invisible, a spirit's voice haunting his unmarked sepulcher. His gaunt face is heavily lined, his expression austere, shoulders stooped, and the top of his head completely bald and speckled with spots from the sun. What is left of his hair has been collected into a long braid which forms a wispy gray rope down his back. He wears a thick brown robe, so long that even his feet are covered. When he turns toward the niche, I see that he holds before him a large tablet of amber, the sacred text he's been reading from encased within it.

A second man joins him at his side, kisses two of his own fingertips, then touches them to the amber. The speaker bows slightly, kneels before the niche, and pushes the tablet into it. Then he sits back onto his heels, and with arms outstretched along the floor begins to mumble inaudibly.

"Peace." The speaker this time is the other man barely perceptible in the lamplight, a man much taller than his elder and with a voice much more resonant. His hair is blond and wavy like his sister's, but cropped short above his ears. His eyes, however, are bigger than hers, and bright cerulean, the color of the Great Sea on clear summer days; they are eyes that pierce right through me.

"Peace," I repeat, unsure if silence would have been the safer response. But the leader smiles and motions for Alexa and me to come nearer.

"Sister," the leader says to Alexa as he bends over to embrace her. "I was up all night long with the priest praying for you. I declared a fast until you returned safely."

"I'm sorry, brother. I can explain everything if you wa – "

"Shhh…" he says, and kisses her forehead. "No explanation is required. All that matters is that you're home now."

Alexa wraps her arms around her brother's torso and squeezes him tightly; then, as if remembering the nuisance standing behind her, she quickly drops her arms and shoots her eyes back at me. "Brother, do you not wish me explain *her*?" she asks.

"This is Acheron's slave?" he asks.

"*Was*," I say, surprised at how much the correction feels like a reflex bursting from my lips. My antipathy toward Acheron seems to be intensifying by the hour…

"Do not speak to my brother unless he asks you to!" Alexa hisses. Her brother smiles and places both his hands on her shoulders.

"It's alright, sister," he says. "I can respect her eagerness to disassociate from her master – *former* master," he grins, flashing an ivory smile that could only be rivaled by one other person I know…

The thought of Tycho's dimpled grin makes me remember Carya's warning to me through Aspasia, that I would find him near the amber scrolls and speak up for his life as he spoke up for mine. But I have heard nothing of Tycho since I sat at Gennadius's table, and I hope with all that I am no rumor of him emerges, because I haven't the slightest idea how I could defend him – and more importantly, if I would even dare to try.

The burden I carry assures me that I have no debts owed to anyone, not even to the man who saved my life. All I have is a chance to avenge my brother and the others who have perished at Acheron's hand. And I'm going to take it.

"My name is Iris, sir," I say, trying pitifully to redeem my first impression.

"I'm Diokles, leader of the Soukinoi." He extends his hand, and I take it.

A palpable silence hangs in the air between us as he continues to grip my hand, not hard, but not softly either, just enough to make me feel vulnerable and hope that his moods are not as erratic as his sister's. I keep my eyes on his, careful not to look away like a cornered animal.

Finally, he lets go.

"It must have been terrifying being a slave to such a monster," he says. "Never knowing when your next whipping might be. Wondering if the next lash will be the last thing you feel..." I nod my head and bite my lip, fighting to resist the stinging memories of midnight beatings and the smell of wine and blood mingling on my lacerated body. "You must be very brave," he says, and then slides a knife out of his belt. "Antipater, you may leave now!"

The old priest slowly peels his arms off the floor and pushes a skeletal hand against the wall as he gets to his feet. His feet make a shuffling sound as he moves like a sloth toward the door. With a groan of exertion he pulls open the door and lets himself out of the cella and into an abrasive rectangle of sun. I close my eyes until the door is shut, which seems like an eternity as I wonder why the priest was told to leave...and why Diokles holds a dagger in his hand...

"My sister doesn't spare just anyone," Diokles says. "Whether she'll admit to it or not, her intuition told her to test you, and to bring you here."

Alexa stares at me blankly, apathetically. Did she really see something valuable in me back in Limén, or was she simply satisfying her thirst for adventure, or indulging her curiosity about my gift? I may never know, but it doesn't matter anyway. All she wants is to please her brother; that much is clear.

"Lysander wanted to kill you because of your loyalty to Acheron," Diokles goes on. "I sent Alexa to kill you in case cowardice got the better of you, which it did." I open my mouth to refute his opinion, but think better of it and bite my tongue. "And both times you have escaped death. I cannot believe that such luck is merely coincidence."

"I want to kill Acheron. I missed my chance because – "

"Because her doma didn't work," Alexa says casually, as if she were referring to a farmer's obstinate ox or a builder's broken hammer.

Diokles's eyes light up. "You're an Asher? You must have just received your impartation."

"And what makes you say that?" I ask, discomfited by his shrewd assumption.

"The fact that you obviously don't know how it operates," he answers. "But I can show you. Do you want to master it?" His lambent eyes dance under the dim yellow light.

I want to avenge my brother, I think.

I answer loudly, calmly, "I've heard you're planning a revolt, and I want to be a part of it."

"Yes, at the Feast of Therismos in Eirene just a few days away. Acheron will be there, along with all the Guardians. And together we will deliver them to Hades, won't we, sister?" he says, squeezing Alexa's shoulder. She jumps up and down, clapping her hands, tickled by the thought of massacre.

"I have my own armor, Iris," she says. "You will be very jealous."

But I'm too excited to be envious. I'm no longer chasing a dream; I've been given a guarantee – a time, a place for my hunt to reach its climax.

"Alexa, the jar," says Diokles. Alexa turns, disappears into the darkness, and returns moments later holding a cloth and a clay jar. Her brother closes his eyes and repeats from memory:

"*The man who holds contempt for the judge or for the priest who stands ministering to Duna shall be put to death. You must expel the evil from Petros.*"

"Give me your right hand." he says, opening his eyes. I give it to him and he turns it palm up, resting the knife blade in its center. "Ah. The power is here. I feel it." He smiles at my hand, then slowly begins wrenching my forearm until I hiss in pain and my agitated veins rise to the surface, pushing my flame-hot skin against his hand.

He jerks his hand back fast, and the knife falls with a sharp ping onto the floor; he shakes his hand cool before picking it up and taking my hand again. "Full of fire, are you, Iris?"

My heartbeat accelerates and I can feel my hand start to sweat inside his grasp. He already knows what I am and what I have, and I know there's no turning back, no changing my mind. *The prophecy said you would end up here,* I hear a voice whisper to me from within. *You mustn't fight your fate.*

"Do you swear to focus the energy of your doma on destroying our oppressors?"

"I do."

"Do you swear never to use your doma against one of your Soukinoi brethren?"

"I do."

"Do you swear to follow the orders you are given without deviation?"

"I do."

Diokles picks up his dagger and stares into my eyes as he drags the blade across my palm. And I don't flinch. I've known pain much worse than this.

Alexa holds the jar below our hands. I tilt mine, watching the wine-red blood spill into it, feeling the throbbing flesh, and letting my lips form a smile as I envision Acheron's life emptying into a vessel of my own.

"It is done," says Diokles. "Welcome, sister."

CHAPTER THIRTEEN
PROMETHEUS

Alexa sits beside me at a sandstone table while we wait for breakfast with at least a hundred others gathered inside this mud brick tavern. The air is thick, the musty smell of barley porridge permeating the cramped space and causing the biggest and hungriest of the Soukinoi to restlessly spin their swords on the earthen floor and throw their daggers into lines of crude wooden targets that wrap the walls. Alexa drums her fingers along the table, humming a made-up melody as she munches on a sweet-smelling piece of fruit.

"The men and women eat together?" I ask her, counting seven other women at our table alone.

"We aren't Alpha," says Alexa. "We're a family. Didn't your family eat together?" I nod and feel myself relax a little as I sit back in my chair.

Alexa reaches across me and takes two dry, pitted dates from a ceramic tray and dips each one into a honey-filled amphora on her left. "Here." She places one in my hand as she sinks her teeth into the other with a sportive smile.

As I thank her, the men in the room begin to whoop as the cooks, four matronly, well-fed-looking women, burst out of the kitchen, each carrying a shallow, black-glazed bowl of porridge. The noise elevates, and it becomes clear that the tables cheering the loudest are served first. The cooks rush back into the kitchen and return again, pink-cheeked but cheerful, with hefty bowls overflowing with barley bread, figs, and olives. I look down at my plate; not a centimeter of it has been left uncovered by food.

From over my shoulder, a man pours water into my cup. "Eat as much as you can. You'll need your strength." The voice belongs to Titus, the Soukinoi general.

"Thank you," I say, taking a drink. "Strength for what?"

"Titus, it's supposed to be a surprise!" Alexa whines, brow knitted, bread crumbs bouncing off her lips.

"I think I've had my fair share of surprises lately," I say. Titus's cheek twitches.

"I think you'll find that Soukinoi life is a continuous stream of surprises," he says.

"Don't ruin it for her! Go on!" orders Alexa, shooing him away like a gnat. Titus takes a breath, retaining his composure against the girl's insolence, and walks away.

"I took the oath," I say to Alexa. "See! Why must I be surprised?" I raise my hand, wrapped in a blood-stained bandage, and steady it in front of her eyes as she swallows a fat fig whole. She starts to choke.

"Didn't your mother teach you to chew your food before you swallowed it?" I joke, enjoying her bout of discomfort.

Alexa coughs until the fig is regurgitated and strikes a fluffy biscuit on her plate.

"And didn't yours teach you not to ruin appetites by waving your bleeding wounds around during meals?!" she retorts. "I was choking because *that* disgusted me." She flicks the tender slice in my hand.

"Whatever you say...princess," I say with an impertinent bow. "Will your majesty ever forgive my boorish, provincial manners?"

Alexa turns to me and takes my hands in her lap, and squeezes them until I wince.

"Listen well, *sister*," she starts. "You know I care nothing for manners, only that my brother's soldiers have enough with which to show some respect. Just because you said a few words and spilled a few drops of blood doesn't make anyone here trust you. Our trust has to be earned."

Alexa throws my hands off her lap as the high-pitched sound of sword blades clanging against each other silences the tavern. We both turn to see Titus standing on the centermost table, sheathing his sword and returning the other to its owner seated below.

"Thank Duna he has given us another day, my brothers and sisters!" he exclaims. The Soukinoi clap and cheer, then begin beating the hilts of their daggers against the tables; here the weapons seem to serve a double function as extra appendages.

"Now let's get on with it! Everybody out except for all psiloi!" Titus yells above the din of energized warriors.

The men and women here may love to revel, but they are not unaccustomed to submitting to authority; we've all lived under the Alphas' boots for too long – taking orders is in our blood. But as I look around at my fellow Soukinoi, I can sense the boiling in their veins, almost hear their fervent heartbeats becoming more rapid, and it strikes me that this entire desert compound is nothing less than a cauldron of that emotion, growing hotter and hotter and bubbling more and more until the day it overflows with scorching violence, making room for a new kind of blood, a free blood...

I push back my chair from the table and stand to leave. Then, taking my cue from the others around me, I collect what bite-sized morsels are left on my plate and stow them into my pouch. Alexa elbows me in the ribs.

"Not *you*," she says. "You're part of the psiloi!"

Psiloi are skilled skirmishers who fight only with daggers or shorts words. Creating chaos is their specialty. Certain I have no choice what my station is to be here under Diokles's jurisdiction, I take my seat again without debate.

After the crowd funnels out of the tavern, Titus steps down from the table and stands before the ten of us who remain. He places his helmet on the nearest table and pulls from his belt a tightly rolled papyrus scroll and begins to open it slowly, carefully, as if his fingertips might cause the fragile thing to burst into flames at any moment.

"What is that?" I whisper to Alexa.

"He's going to tell us what our mission is. I don't know why he needs one of the old Alpha scrolls to do it, though," she says, well above a whisper.

The other psiloi, uneager to indulge the general's desire to read from a rotting manuscript that reeks of pagan lore, begin to murmur.

Titus clears his throat. The murmuring stops.

"Diokles gave express orders that this be read to you before your next mission," he says.

"This scroll records one of the first Alpha myths to ever tarnish this world with its noxious lies and blasphemy. It is perhaps the last copy in existence. We keep it here not to honor it, but to revile it. To let it remind us of the evil against which we war. To fan the flames of righteous anger within us lest they be extinguished through carelessness and complacency."

Titus's eyes look straight into mine, then move from psilos to psilos seated around me, kindling the embers within each one of us.

"Read it, Titus!" shouts Alexa. Her fellow fighters drum the table in unison, their fires raging once again.

Titus shuts his eyes and bows his head.

"Almighty Duna, your name means Power, and we acknowledge that all the might and strength and power we possess flows through your hands to ours. Take these fictitious lines of evil and use them to produce in us an unquenchable thirst to avenge your holy name and restore goodness to our land."

His eyes open and fall upon the scroll. He begins to read:

"Prometheus, great Titan god, a prophet of guile and grace,
You took pity upon humanity and defied Zeus to his face.
When you brought fire down from heaven, you supplied mankind with power;
The moment history crowned you Hero became your darkest hour.
For Hephaestus chained you to a cliff, and then did Zeus deliver
A ravenous eagle to attend your side, gnawing always at your liver."

I watch Alexa as her mouth hangs agape, its corners pulled slightly upward into a puckish smile; I'm sure the gruesome image is one she'd love to see up close...

Titus lifts his eyes and begins rolling the scroll back up again.

"I won't go on," he says. "There isn't any need – "

The psiloi interrupt his words with dissenting groans, craving more of the macabre mythic tale. I find myself joining in, hoping to hear how terribly poor Prometheus was made to suffer...and if he was ever given pardon.

Is the Alpha's Zeus a god of forgiveness as our Duna is said to be?

"Nor is there any time!" Titus yells.

The grumbling trails off as all eyes watch our leader walk to a shadowy table in the corner and retrieve from it a small clay tablet. He carries it back to us, protectively holding it against his chest so that our curious eyes cannot pick out a single letter.

"I read to you of the grim fate of Prometheus because that is the fate our judge has sentenced for a traitor close to our midst," explains Titus.

Our silence urges him to go on.

"This man is a priest at an oasis eight miles north of our station here. His beliefs and those of his followers stand in direct opposition to our own."

The hilts of knives begin to beat thunderously against the tables.

"They want us to lay down our swords and devote our days to prayer. They want us to tame our tongues and speak only of a nebulous peace that never comes. They want us to avert our gaze from injustices and blasphemy and pretend none of it exists..."

The psiloi cannot contain their indignation and begin to hiss and bellow curses. Some stand in their chairs and drive their swords and daggers toward the sky, ready to journey north at this very moment.

"Who is this man?" demands Alexa. "And what is his fate?"

Titus opens his mouth to answer, but hesitates, staring down at his boots. Then slowly, he looks up and turns the tablet toward us, revealing the name of the Soukinoi's next target:

Ειρηναίος.

"Ireneus is his name," he says, quickly ridding his lips of the words like rotten food.

The noise dies suddenly. Every sword and dagger lowers. Even Alexa sits still, and speechless, and I wonder what it is I'm missing.

"Ireneus?" questions a psilos to my left. "He's a Eusebian, a great – a great student of the Oracles..." His sentence stumbles, then fades into a dead end of confusion.

"Yes. It is the same man," confirms Titus. "With this mission, Diokles desires to make it known that the Soukinoi will not tolerate heretical leaders, not even those who are among our own people."

Titus looks at me again. From beneath his tough soldier's shell, I see the faraway look of sorrow emanating from his copper eyes. Perhaps he cannot be surprised, but he *can* be moved, even if it is only to pause and consider the cost of war, to let his heart be rent, just for a second, as he realizes how easily, how insidiously, it can turn a people against itself.

His eyes still on mine, Titus discloses the rest of Diokles's plan:

"Our judge commands that our most recent oath-taker, Iris, unleash the traitor's punishment: a Gryphon to rip Ireneus limb from limb."

"Are you surprised?" Alexa whispers.

I have no response for her, only a vacant stare produced by the lukewarm emptiness floating in my veins - neither hot nor cold, neither impassioned nor antagonistic. I feel only stagnant ambivalence, the sense of being swept into the action of a dream, the battles of which I've been content to experience vicariously through unconscious specter's eyes, but must now don armor for, and find out it is no dream at all.

CHAPTER FOURTEEN
GRYPHON

A psilos named Lycus is assigned to lead our mission. We follow him in somber silence up the Serpent's Path which winds laboriously from the desert floor to the imposing peak of Ēlektōr's summit four-hundred meters above. I was told by Alexa that the plateau itself is the Soukinoi fortress. The temple, she said, "is retribution for the Alphas. They defiled the Temple in Eirene with their unclean sacrifices; we will create catacombs of theirs, filled with the bones of their Guardians."

My blood races as I think of Acheron, whose bones I will soon bury there.

An hour into the ascent, I hear the shrill, ear-splitting sound of an eagle calling from the heights above. We all press our fingers against our ears, but the cacophonous song of the Gryphon still slips through.

"Hear that, Iris?" yells Alexa. "She beckons you!"

"Why doesn't your brother have the apostate priest tied to a stake right here? That wretched sound is torture enough!" I yell back, my head feeling as though it could explode if the piping notes continue much longer. The other psiloi laugh until a cascade of wind comes rushing down the mountain.

Lycus trudges on, holding his cloak before him as a shield. I feel coarse grains of sand begin to hit my face and pull my cloak up as well, sacrificing my ears to the Gryphon's unbearable keening.

At last, we reach a massive wall made of unwrought limestone boulders. In its center is the threshold to the fortress, a stone portal measuring at least ten feet wide and ten feet high. Above the lentil stretches a long slab supporting a triangular relief of two stone gryphons that face each other with unfurled wings and frightful wide-open beaks. Two watchtowers stand across from one another on either side of the gate; a pair of sentry eyes looks down on us from each one.

The sentry closest to the gate signals to some unseen guard below, and moments later the giant double door opens. Lycus nods at the guard above and in we go, closer to the thing emitting those accursed shrieks. But as we enter the gates, the Gryphon goes silent, perhaps placated by the discovery that the ten psiloi it spied half an hour before are not trespassers, but unannounced guests.

The plateau is a small city unto itself, replete with storehouses, pigeon coops, barracks, an armory, and cisterns filled with rainwater. Around us, hundreds of Soukinoi men and women go about their duties like diligent bees buzzing about a hive. A group of women gathers water and returns it to their living quarters between the walls surrounding the fortress. Teenaged boys covered in coal dust carry mud bricks and hammers into a nearby smithy, while younger brown-skinned boys sit atop wooden crates chiseling arrowheads in the sun.

Just half a mile from the gates lies an immense palace that is situated strategically on the westernmost edge, overlooking the desert like an impenetrable cloud bank hovering high on Mount Olympus. Staring up at the palace's courtyard walls, I notice the rounded iron dome of a colossal structure perfectly resembling a birdcage.

Cages that big do not exist, I think.

Then I see a gigantic, piercing yellow eye press itself firmly against the bars to get a better look at its visitors, and suddenly I am thankful for whoever forged that gargantuan cage.

We enter the courtyard and regard the ancient winged creature, one of the few still soaring the skies of Petros, and doing the bidding of both Python and the Alphas' most powerful men. But now, I see, even a few bold Eusebians have managed to conscribe one for their own clandestine purposes.

The Gryphon must be no shorter than twelve feet. Its two rear feet are like a lion's, tawny, broad, and heavy-looking, while its forefeet are that of an eagle's, vivid orange and tipped with black, razor-sharp talons. The animal sits motionless upon a wooden platform that stretches the length of the cage; all that moves is its tufted, leonine tail hanging below the platform, swinging languidly from side to side in a smooth, hypnotic rhythm.

Lycus and another of the psiloi, the strongest of the bunch, step forward and stand to the right of the cage's enormous log which serves as a latch across the door frame.

Please don't open that.

"Great Gryphon, I am Lycus, captain in the Soukinoi army of Diokles!" Lycus announces, bowing his head in obeisance to the formidable bird.

The Gryphon's tail ceases its swinging as two charcoal wings start to twitch and rouse out of their dormancy. The creature cocks her snow-white head toward Lycus, and I watch as a thin, translucent membranous lid slides across each of her eyes; when the lids recede, the bird expels a blaring shriek that reverberates inside my chest and creates goose bumps on my flesh. I lean against the wall as the Gryphon's wings break away violently from its body, the full span of them cut short by the cage's rattling bars.

Not to be made a mouse of this hostile half-lion, Lycus lifts his chin and places his hands on a cage bar. The Gryphon tilts her head curiously and jumps down from the platform onto the lowest level to inspect this brave interlocutor. Her hooked yellow beak slowly descends upon Lycus's hands and presses against them...a subservient kiss...

The eight of us stand in a line along the wall, not talking, not even Alexa. All of our eyes are locked on the awesome animal and the privileged colloquy she appears to be having with our captain. Though the bird doesn't speak, she seems to register every word Lycus says, responding with an intelligent nod of her head, an excited flutter of her wings, a favorable wave of her tail.

After a few minutes, Lycus motions to the stout psiloi standing nearby and together they lift the log and drag it forcefully away from the door frame.

The Gryphon pounces out of her lair like a lion, then takes to the skies like an eagle, gliding and diving and drifting through the bright blue dome of Petros, relishing her freedom from iron bars. I wonder how she came to serve the Soukinoi, and why she chooses not to fly back to her former territory and leave us, the desert zealots, without our foremost weapon.

Perhaps she enjoys being the weapon, I think.

As the Gryphon makes her descent, I am convinced that my hypothesis is correct. As she lowers her head, arches her wings, and reaches her talons for the sand, she lets out an exhilarated shriek, and I know that I am looking not upon an enslaved animal made to murder against its will, but an amenable assassin who lives to savor the taste of death.

One of the psiloi at the end of our line pulls the sack off his shoulder and carries it toward the Gryphon. The bird, evidently familiar with this particular soukinos, leaps toward him, causing him to jump back in fear.

Before his shaky fingers can pull open the bag, the Gryphon's beak is plunging into it, edaciously removing slimy strings of sepia-colored earthworms and eating them whole. I cringe as I see the scale-covered, white and black body of a viper drop from the writhing cluster of worms.

It slithers only a few feet toward the nearest shadow before the Gryphon's paw thwarts its escape with a hard, merciless stomp. Her beak whips the snake off the ground, swings and shakes it like a child's plaything, then swallows it down with a satisfied cackle.

"I'm supposed to control this animal?" I whisper to Alexa beside me. She points her finger toward the eastern wing of the palace, and I see Lycus and his helper emerging from it, their arms draped with thick leather straps and a metal, basket-like device filled with holes.

I give Alexa an inquisitive look, but, clearly amused by my show of ignorance, she offers no explanation, only smiles haughtily.

The Gryphon chirps happily as she sees Lycus and the strong psiloi approaching her. She retracts her claws and lowers her head onto the sand as if in surrender to our puny army. The two men begin pulling the metal apparatus onto the Gryphon's face, and I realize that they are muzzling her. They attach the leather straps to either side of the muzzle and slide the reins over the monster's neck. Then Lycus turns to me.

"Iris. Today you are the Gryphon's keeper," he says. "This is her first mission in a very long time. You should feel honored."

I don't move a muscle. I don't make a sound. Not until Alexa pushes me forward.

"Wha – what am I to do, Lycus?" the words tumble out of me.

"The Gryphon knows what to do. All *you* must do is pretend you are Athena, goddess of justice," he smiles. "We will meet you there to take care of the others."

The psiloi laugh as Lycus bids me come closer. He kneels, interlaces his fingers to form a step for my foot, then helps me onto the Gryphon's back.

"And hold on tight."

I take the reins as Lycus yells, "Away!" sending the Gryphon lunging up and into the air and my body backwards, sliding toward the tip of her right wing.

"I said hold on tight!" Lycus calls out.

The Gryphon screeches and tilts right until she is nearly perpendicular to the ground, her flight frustrated by the full weight of my body hanging onto her feathers. Knowing better than to look down, I pull and kick and claw my way back up, settling myself in between her shoulders.

The Gryphon rights herself and continues climbing, climbing, climbing, higher and higher like Icarus speeding toward the sun. And when I think of how Icarus met his end, dead in the sea with melted wings, I shut my eyes.

After a few seconds, I am calm enough to open my eyes. I look down and see the desert shrinking below me, the fortress shriveling to the size of a sandcastle as a pure blue curtain of sky envelops me. The shouts of the Soukinoi quickly evanesce within the voiceless bliss high above the world, a region reserved solely for the freest of creatures, the ones whose messages to each other and the rest of creation are transmitted through song. I hear only the wind singing to me now, whooshing over my head and shoulders, pulling my skin tight against my face as it intones the rhythm of the Gryphon's dipping and rising.

I release the reins, close my eyes again, and stretch out my arms, imagining them to be mighty Gryphon wings, imagining myself to be free of my allegiance to anyone or anything...save for the unbreakable oath to avenge my brother.

CHAPTER FIFTEEN
KILLER

We reach the Oasis of Éleos far before the other psiloi who travel behind on foot. The Gryphon takes us to a secluded aerie she knows high upon a rose-colored mountain. I slide off her wing and move carefully to the edge of the cliff for a better view of the misty waterfall and lush green haven below, all of it atwitter with the lively pips of sandpipers and wood warblers. The Gryphon lies down in her nest, shuts her eyes, and bows her head. Eat, sleep, fly, and kill. That is the life she knows.

⸺⟨⟨⟩⟩⸺

It isn't until I hear the harmonious sound of singing voices climbing toward us that I realize that I, too, have been sleeping.

The Gryphon's wings clap open as she jumps to her feet and alerts me with a deep, guttural growl, softened by the muzzle enwrapping her jaws. I raise my hand at the Gryphon, signaling her to be quiet, and creep slowly across the crunching nest until I reach a boulder to hide behind, letting my heartbeat slow to match the soothing cadence of the chorus below.

Phos, son of Duna, creator of light, giver of love,
You dove into Petros' sea of plight, stepped out of the streams of life above.
Phos, son of Duna, defeater of Python, sender of hope,
You set the Moonbow in our skies; your grace transcends our finite scope.
Phos, son of Duna, you were obedient unto death,
We will praise and serve you until our final mortal breath.

Obedient unto death.

The line rolls over me like a wave as I think of Jasper singing the same song the last time we were together, just days before his arrest. We'd spent the afternoon visiting the graves of our parents, graves that were marked modestly by the violet bouquets of irises we carried there week after week throughout the spring and summer months.

Obedient unto death.

Even then, before my brother's execution and my own enslavement, I had trouble making sense of those words. I couldn't fathom how a divine being so powerful could be slain...or how his infallible father Duna could allow it.

"Phos gave his life willingly, entered into the abyss of the Great Sea so that you and I never have to," Jasper had tried to explain to me after I'd asked him where he thought our parents' spirits had gone...if anywhere.

"Mother and father rejoiced at the Moonbow's appearing. They knew Phos was who he claimed to be. I feel I've been called to share the good news with all of Petros, Iris. Wherever Duna leads me. Beginning with you."

I can see his face so clearly. The way his tranquil gray eyes smiled as he spoke. The soft blue circles beneath them formed by sleepless nights spent on his knees in prayer alongside others like him.

"I always pray for you, my sister. I always will," he'd said.

I know little of Ireneus, but his shared beliefs with my brother are enough for me to know that I cannot have a hand in his death.

The singing stops on the path below. A man yells, then yells again:

"Gryphon! The Gryphon!"

I turn to see the Gryphon facing the noise with wings pulled high and rearward, forming a black feathered wall that blocks the sun and draws all eyes to hers, which now glow luminously with an infernal spark that sends my hand straight to my dagger. But what can I do to her?

Don't do this, Gryphon!

"Ready your weapons! Ireneus, your sword!" I hear the voice command.

The Gryphon's head lowers, her burning yellow eyes boring into my skull. With just one look, I can read her thoughts, and I don't doubt she can read mine...

I want to be rid of this monster and hand her reins to another psiloi, one who is desensitized to this barbarism, to the ruthless judgments of non-existent gods come to life.

Sensing my trepidation, the Gryphon hops toward me, wild eyes pleading with me to remove the muzzle, to get on with this mission and make a meal of this traitorous priest, Ireneus.

The footsteps grow closer. They will see me soon, and what then?

Let the Gryphon do her work, I think. *Prolong this anymore and you will both be dead before nightfall.*

"Who are you?" I hear a voice ask me.

I turn to see the long slender face of an old man looking down at me, eyes filled with concern. He steps around the boulder, holding up his sword with both hands toward the Gryphon. I can see by his flowing white robes and multicolored turban that this is none other than the priest.

The Gryphon furiously flaps her wings and half flies, half jumps from one side of her nest to the other.

"You're safe now," says the priest, lending me a hand and helping me to my feet.

Three of the priest's disciples arrive and catch their breaths. They too raise their swords to the Gryphon and eye me with suspicion.

"Who is she?" one of them asks.

"That's the Gryphon of Diokles! We must kill it, master!" shouts another. "The girl is from Ēlektōr!"

Ireneus looks at me questioningly for a moment, then places his hand on my shoulder and whispers for only me to hear, "Daughter, would you like to come with us? It isn't too late."

"Do you swear to follow the orders you are given without deviation?" Diokles's words materialize in my mind like a sudden patch of fog. I know that to harm the Gryphon, or impede her, will surely mean my own traitor's death.

"Please," I whisper. "Run now. As fast as you can!" I start walking backwards toward the Gryphon, waving the priest away with hands that grow hotter by the second.

The animal rushes to me and throws her neck down at my feet, begging me to free her. I place my fingers over the bronze muzzle and let them hover there, watching the back of the animal quickly rise and fall with each turbulent breath, and waiting for I don't know what. I look up at Ireneus, who slowly begins to back away.

"Do it, Iris!" It's Alexa's voice. But I don't know where it's coming from. "Release her!"

Knowing Lycus and the others must be close by, I unfasten the muzzle and am thrust back into the nest as the Gryphon bolts past me and charges the priest, her curved talons reaching toward him, then knocking him into the boulder with a bone-breaking thud.

"No!" With my scream flies a single fireball from my right hand. It zooms like a flash of white lightning toward the beast, missing her head by inches, then slams into the boulder, forming a foot-long fissure and filling it with smoke. The Gryphon turns to me, her yellow eyes ablaze, and pipes her displeasure with me in loud, scraping squawks. I press my wrists to my ears and feel the intense heat of my hands encircling my head, chastising me for missing my mark.

Shuddering, I watch as Ireneus's body goes limp like a ragdoll, white robes crumpling as he slouches and falls to his side, sword slipping out of his right hand into the dust.

Ireneus's three followers run at the Gryphon and wave their swords like mad men, then make threatening jabs toward the bird's tree-like legs.

"Alexa?!" I yell. The Gryphon cocks her head at me. The men stop and look at me, bemused, then quickly glance around them and resume their fighting stances.

Where are the others?! I think.

I stand up and begin to walk around the nest's perimeter to see if I can spot the other psiloi somewhere down the mountain. But after only a few steps, the Gryphon's wings pop open again, this time forming a warning, a barrier, to keep me locked inside her lair.

She lets out a high, victorious shriek and ducks her head toward the ground. I watch in horror as Ireneus's unconscious body is dragged away by the bloodthirsty scavenger. Shutting my eyes and covering my ears, I try to ignore the outcry of the three left standing, but after a minute or less, their shouting stops.

I open my eyes, but there is nothing to see, only Ireneus's sword half-hidden in the boulder's shadow. I go to it and pick it up, then cautiously step around the rock and gaze down the mountain until the weight of what I see takes the air out of my lungs and steals the ground under my feet.

There, in the midst of the sun-bathed path, lie the four blood-soaked bodies of Ireneus and his disciples being pecked and prodded by the Gryphon's crimson beak.

I hear myself scream as I will myself off the ground and dash back up the path toward the aerie. If I try to run elsewhere, I fear the Gryphon will warn me no more, and then it will be my entrails she's feasting on.

"Iris! Girl, where are you going?" I turn to see Lycus shouting at me from below, just a few feet from the Gryphon who pays him no mind as she continues to gorge herself. "You can come down now!"

I make haste down the path, carefully gripping Ireneus's sword and averting my eyes from the carnage of the Gryphon's kill. Waiting for me are all ten of my fellow psiloi who synchronously lower their heads in respect, even Alexa.

"What have you got there?" asks Lycus, looking at the sword.

"It belonged to Ireneus," I say.

Lycus looks pleased and begins to say something when Alexa interjects.

"I didn't think you had it in you!" she says. Then she turns to the others, pumps her petite fist in the air and leads the group as they cry out:

"Victory rewards the brave! Victory rewards the brave!"

I smile, but it is by no means a proud smile or a thankful smile, but a troubled one, a primal reaction formed by agitated nerves and twitching muscles. I hurry toward Lycus whose greedy arms and triumphant eyes reach out for the martyr's sword.

"Well done," he commends me, taking the sword. "We looked for the priest down at the oasis and feared he might have migrated back west toward civilization."

"He asked me if I wanted to go with him," I confess, my voice devoid of emotion, though my soul feels thick with it.

"You made the right choice," he says.

Alexa skips over to join us and takes me by the hand, her blond hair and pretty, nymph-like smile the perfect façade to mask her nefarious nature.

"Now I know," she chirps, "you truly are a sister."

"Where were you earlier?" I ask. "When I called for you."

"What do you mean? I've been with Lycus and the others taking care of the rest of Ireneus's men," she says.

"But I heard you up on the mountain. You yelled at me to let the Gryphon go. I heard you…"

Alexa looks at me as though I've become the Hydra and sprouted eight heads.

"Sister, I assure you it wasn't me." She puts her hands to my cheeks. "You feel a little warm. Perhaps you're becoming ill… You have a weak stomach, perhaps?" she grins.

"Alexa has been with us, Iris," Lycus attests. "I would wager the voice you heard was your own conscience speaking to you. And you did right to listen to it."

I feel my stomach tighten, my lip and brow become dotted with sweat as I hear another voice, an inner voice, whispering clearly:

You are listening to fools!

A gray tunnel quickly encloses my vision, growing darker and darker until all light and every sound are sucked out, and all I can feel is the profound sensation of dread paralyzing my body and tormenting my mind.

CHAPTER SIXTEEN
INTERVENTION

I wake up inside a sandstone cave, one of dozens that honeycomb the mountains surrounding the Soukinoi camp. Alexa and five other women are curled up close together like cats against the walls, their weapons heaped one on top of the other in the middle of the space. I feel a damp cloth pressed against my forehead and notice a half-empty cup near the wall on my right. I pick it up and detect the spicy scent of ginger root, and I wonder if it was Alexa, my new "sister," who tended to me after my world went black atop the mountain.

My stomach is no longer in knots, my face no longer perspires, but the ache in my soul still persists, and I fear it will linger until the fresh images of the Gryphon's slaughter dim in the remotest recesses of my mind. Or, perhaps, until I become callous toward the sight of such brutality and learn not to question the means by which we obtain victory.

"We make war that we may live in peace," I whisper to myself, hoping these words of a long-dead Petrodian sage will restore mettle to my mind, and zeal to my soul so the doma will operate as it should.

I crawl to the cave's edge and lean against the wall, watching the purple cloak of night tear into pieces, breaking apart beneath the fiery touch of sunrise.

⚜

Water has never felt so wonderful. Not even in the desert when my throat was parched and my light skin burned. As I wade in the hot pool inside the bathhouse, I shut my eyes and try to imagine the filth and guilt and blood of yesterday being washed away from my body. The temperature of this pool is too scalding for most of the Soukinoi, but to me, it feels perfect. I feel purged...cleansed. The inner aching ceases.

I lie on my back on top of the water and let the feeling of weightlessness lull me to the verge of sleep. I hear the muffled conversation and splashing of horseplay of the Soukinoi in the pools adjacent to mine, but I am content not to fraternize or talk of last night's killing. All I want to do is let my memories of the mission slough off from my skin like a layer of grime and sink to the bottom of this pool.

"Soukina!"

As soon as I finally feel at ease, I am jolted out of my daze by a man's resounding shout and the sound of his sandals slapping across the stone floor.

"Iris, care to join us?"

Above me stands Diokles with an amused look on his face as he waves at the three men accompanying him to pass by, one of whom wears a sackcloth bag over his head...and a Pythonian tattoo on his right forearm...

"Uh, yes – yes, sir!" I say, standing to my feet and nervously twisting the water out of my heavy hair.

"You did well yesterday. I pray the ordeal wasn't *too* much for you to endure." He says, his sardonic tone indicating that he knows I was ill.

"I've endured worse," I reply, fighting the urge to cast a glance at the tattooed man. "I think the Gryphon and I could become great friends," I lie. In truth, I would rather meet Acheron's whip seven straight nights than consort with that loathsome beast again.

"Very good. You have surpassed my sister's expectations. And that is no small feat," he grins. "Here, let me help you out of there."

Diokles moves to the pool's steps, bends forward and extends his hand.

"Thank you," I say, letting him pull me out. "I hope I have surpassed your expectations as well."

"You will find that my expectations are never *exceeded*, sister. No Soukinos I have ever trained has proven as passionate, as unflinching as I," he says, still gripping my hand, his head close to mine as he stares into my eyes as if waiting for me to recoil.

But I don't. I stare back stubbornly with as much fervor as I can muster, feeling the solacing droplets of water covering my skin evaporate one by one into the sultry air of the bathhouse.

"You can consider that a challenge," he smiles again as he releases my tingling hand, then strides off toward the others bathing and merrymaking nearby.

I follow after him and sit on the nearest corner of the crowded colder pool, letting my legs dangle casually in the water, hoping that the tattooed prisoner presently being escorted to Diokles's side is nobody I know.

"Soukinoi!" shouts our leader.

Stillness ripples through the bathhouse. The carefree chatter fades to curious whispers, and then to steady breath upon the waves. Diokles waits until every last echo has died to proceed with his announcement.

"Many of you know the man standing here before you. Although, to call him a man is to elevate him high above his rightful rank among Duna's hierarchy of creatures, for he is no more than a maggot, a traitor to Python, a traitor to us... A true man would have made up his mind whose side he was on by now, wouldn't you agree, soldiers?!"

The bathhouse erupts in a discordant blend of booing, laughing, hissing, applauding until Diokles raises his hand and presses a finger to his lips. Without saying another word, he inches closer to the covered man and swiftly pulls the bag off of his head with such force that the prisoner loses his balance and falls headlong into the pool.

I hear Alexa's shrill, girlish laughter ringing out over the crowd, and then a collective gasp as the man emerges from the water, pushing his black hair back from his eyes.

Tycho!

My first impulse is to slide into the pool and conceal myself among the small sea of soldiers. My warm body stings as it's plunged to the throat in ice-cold water. I wait for myself to adjust to it, but I never do; the stinging subsides, but I'm still left shaking. I'm completely scared stiff. I can almost sense the temperature in the bathhouse rising ten degrees as blood runs hot and muscles tense.

It takes several minutes for the hellish sounds of a viper's nest to hush and for the riled waves to ebb again. When they do, Diokles motions to his two guards. They swoop down on Tycho like eagles, grab him by his underarms, and then lean back, planting their feet firmly as though dragging him up out of the water will require all their strength.

But Tycho needn't be forced. He calmly helps himself onto the edge, stands, shakes his sandals, takes his place between the guards, and looks out into every eye he can find to connect with. He's clearly not ashamed, and curiously, not afraid. I hear the sentries grunt, expressing their displeasure in finding that their prisoner hasn't got any fight in him. At least not anymore.

"A peacemaker is what he may prefer you to call him!" resumes Diokles. "But again, we would be flattering this man, this once-fearless warrior, by granting him such a...*diplomatic* title. We shall call him what he truly is, what he was all along: a worthless, spineless parasite." Diokles spits on Tycho's toes. "For he has, to this moment, used impressive cunning to feed off of a false allegiance to both Python and the Soukinoi!"

Tycho's lips remain closed, his gaze set steadfastly upon his accuser.

Has he gone deaf?! Why doesn't he defend himself? I think.

But I think again: *What good would it do if he did...*

"Each of you!" Diokles shouts. "Hold out your right hand."

The sound of whishing water fills the space as each of us pulls our hand fast out of the pool and wait, like servants, for further instruction.

"Turn it over and look down at the line drawn across it. No matter how faint or fresh it is, no matter if you received it one year ago or yesterday, that is the scar that commemorates the day you swore your oath here, the day you heard me speak these words:

"*The man who holds contempt for the judge or for the priest who stands ministering to Duna shall be put to death.*'"

I unwrap the bandage from around my palm and see that an ugly scab has formed. Soon the wound will scar and I too will bear a permanent mark of loyalty, just like the rest of the Soukinoi. Just like Tycho, just like the Centaur. The only difference between the Soukinoi and Pythonian emblems is that the former is forged with a knife and a little blood, the latter with dye and a sharpened stick.

As I stare at my hand I remind myself that the oath I made in that pagan temple is a means to an end. A necessary rite. The reason I am here is not to get involved in quarrels about war, religion, or politics, but to stay sharp, act brave, and keep out of Diokles's way until I am led to Acheron.

You cannot let Tycho die as you let Ireneus! A voice inside me – my conscience? – startles me. My eyes jump back to Diokles and the man who saved my life.

"This man Tycho is guilty of breaking his oath. He will be stoned at the temple steps at dusk," Diokles says in such a matter-of-fact fashion that I am almost reminded of...

No, not Acheron. Acheron kills without just cause! I reason.

It isn't just to let your friend die, a voice says again.

I feel my soul warring against itself, one side rallying my wits to hold back and play dumb, the other appealing to my heart, something I wish I couldn't feel.

The voice is soft but clear, subtle but undeniable as it reminds me of Carya's prophecy to Aspasia:

"...it shall be your turn to speak up for his life."

My heart jumps into my throat, followed by a stream of words that I can't possibly suppress a moment longer.

"Wait! Diokles! Wait!" I climb out of the pool and run to our leader's side before anyone can stop me.

"Iris!" I hear Alexa gasp as the rest of the Soukinoi look on in astonishment.

"Diokles, forgive me, but Tycho is the one who saved me from Lysander. He is the reason I am here. If I have not proven myself a worthy recruit, then please, take his life. And punish me as you see fit for what I know you consider unforgivable brazenness and – "

"Stop this!" shouts Diokles. His echo repeats the command several times as he turns his back to the Soukinoi and walks slowly closer to me, his hands interlaced behind his back, his teeth clenched together as he whispers:

"You don't know anything about me. But know this. I will not tolerate having my authority publicly undermined by a woman who thinks herself Duna's gift to us just because she survived a single mission!"

I cannot keep my eyes on his, and look down as I mutter a pathetic apology and try to hold back my tears like a scorned child.

"Look at me, Soukina," Diokles says with a softened tone. "I think you are very brave. But do not forget your place. There is a fine line between courage and stupidity."

Diokles turns back to the crowd who has begun to dry themselves off and wring out the water from their garments. I glance over at Tycho but his eyes are closed, his lips moving.

"Tycho showed mercy for our sister, Iris," Diokles says. "I too will show mercy and allow him to live here and render to us his knowledge and skills as a warrior and strategist."

The Soukinoi mumble, and I see Alexa's eyes widen with incredulity.

"But!" continues Diokles. "Should he retaliate, try to flee, or should he speak one word of peacemaking or voice one dissenting opinion about our operations here, he will be stoned."

Diokles returns to my side and puts his hand on my shoulder.

"And she will die in the same manner as her first target, the priest Ireneus."

CHAPTER SEVENTEEN
RENEGADE

I looked for Tycho in the tavern at breakfast, but he was nowhere to be found. I spent the morning ascending the mountain, and by noon I was still wandering about the plateau, ducking into the dwellings hidden between the walls, bothering the blacksmiths as they stoked their fires with billows and beat their hammers against metal. I didn't care if I was intruding into their homes or disrupting their work – I have to find Tycho, and I'm not even sure why. To thank him for saving my life? Maybe. But I know deep down what draws me to him is utterly indefinable: it's the mystery concealed in the sun-streaked pools of his eyes, the serpent tattoo now symbolizing his worst regret, the peace he possessed as Diokles pronounced his death sentence, the way my veins stir with a different kind – a pleasant and benign kind – of heat when I think of him for too long...

"I don't know where he is, but I wish he were in Hades!" was one man's gruff reply at breakfast.

The mere mention of Tycho makes most people's lips curl in disgust before they spit or curse his name. Others shrug their shoulders insouciantly and go about their business; even if they had seen him, I'm sure they wouldn't tell me.

Finally, I arrive at a small, abandoned-looking assembly place located at the southernmost end of the fortress and spot Tycho kneeling there along the highest tier of plastered benches. His eyes are closed, head slightly bowed, still as a clay statue left to dry in the sun.

"Tycho!" I call out to him. But he doesn't move. "Tycho!" I repeat. This time, all I hear in response is the distant, hungry howl of the Gryphon.

Instantly, Ireneus and the three picked-apart, blood-drained bodies of his disciples flash before my mind's eye. I race up the tiers toward Tycho, hoping the exertion will circumvent the formation of another haunting image, that of vibrant red ribbons of torn-apart flesh falling from the Gryphon's beak: the remnants of *my* mangled body, dissected at the order of Diokles.

"You must be starved!" I shout at him, wondering if he'll remember causing me to jump with those words the day he surprised me at the Port of Ourania.

Tycho doesn't jump. He's heard me calling. He opens his eyes after a few seconds and acknowledges my presence with a tired smile.

"And you must have found the work you were looking for. As a tanner, if I recall correctly?"

His smile struggles to linger a while longer, but soon disappears, replaced by a heaviness that fills his eyes; it's as though each one contains an anchor connected to the deepest layer of his soul, and he is unable to cut them loose and sail beyond them.

"I almost began assisting a tanner," I start to explain. "In Limén."

Tycho turns to me and searches my eyes, and all he can say is, "My lady..."

Those words crawl over my skin like a scared spider. I am no more a lady than Alexa, a girl who thrives on mischief, and with a bloodlust to rival the Gryphon's.

"Why didn't you stay there?" Tycho manages, his question sounding more like a plea for me to travel back in time to Gennadius's tannery, stay put in the shadows until the time comes to defend myself – and *only* myself – and forget the Soukinoi altogether.

"The girl who appeared to you gave a message to the tanner's wife. She told me I would come here. And that – *that I would speak up for your life* like you did for mine. Did I have a choice?"

"We all have a choice," he says, anger welling in his voice. "Duna sees your heart. He knows what losing your family and serving Acheron have done to it..."

Tycho clenches his jaw, then looks to the sky. I follow his eyes and watch the white puffs of clouds floating above us, like giant breaths caught in a clear, cold day.

"He is outside the clouds, Iris. He is beyond the Moonbow, beyond time," he continues, his anger carried away into the clouds. "The prophecy didn't send you here. Duna knew you would follow your heart."

"*Your desert journey shall be paved with stones of black desire,*" I say, slowly repeating the verse of Aspasia's prophecy as it moves forward from memory to mouth.

"The tanner's wife told you that, I suppose?"

I nod.

"You would have been safe there. The prophecy could have been different," says Tycho, standing and dusting the sand from his knees.

"I don't want to be safe!" I say as Tycho makes his way down the shallow tiers. "Where are you going?!"

"You want your brother to have vengeance. You want to kill Acheron. I know, Iris. And I know it is foolishness. I'm going to Eirene, and you are welcome to come with me."

"Now who is foolish?!" I yell as I run after him. "Did you hear Diokles this morning, or were you still under water? You will be stoned and I will be eaten alive by the Gryphon if we try to run away!"

Tycho stops and turns to me, then waits for a moment as if deciding whether to say:

"I want to show you something."

He continues walking around the limestone wall until we come upon one of Diokles's chief guards slumped against it. His ghost-pale skin and half-opened eyes indicate that he isn't napping. And when I see the dark red spot soaked into his thigh, I know without question that he is dead.

My eyes grow wide. My heart flutters as I battle the impulse to flee and report the murderer or stay and hear him out. I take a deep breath. I decide to stay.

"I prayed that he would spend his last minutes repenting before Duna. Sometimes the moments preceding death are the only ones men take to think on things that matter..." Tycho says, bearing the same look of compassion that he had at Okeanos when he described Jasper's death to Lysander and the outlaws...as he saved my life...

"Why did you have to kill him?" I demand, frustration squelching any feelings of affection and causing my voice to quiver.

"Diokles sent him, Iris. He *wanted* me to kill him."

"What? You're not any making sense!" I say, feeling my muscles warm with exasperation.

"Mercy was never his intention. He wants me dead, but not now; now he has another idea in mind."

"And what idea is that?"

"He wants to prove to the rest of his followers that he was right about me and that you were wrong....that I am a traitor, a Eusebian-killer..."

"You were defending yourself," I say, putting the pieces together in my mind.

Tycho doesn't answer, but instead leans over the soldier and gently closes his eyes with the palm of his hand.

"Be in peace," Tycho whispers to him.

"Diokles sacrificed one of his own sentries just to set you up?" I ask, wanting to be told differently. But I know that I am right, and Tycho knows I don't really need an answer.

"His men will find him within the hour, and then they will arrest me and make a public spectacle of me, an example of what becomes of renegades."

I wait for Tycho to continue and surmise what they will do with me. But he only looks out over the wall in silence.

"And me?" I ask, a tear rolling down my cheek into the corner of my mouth. The saltiness, the unmistakable taste of vulnerability and brokenness, signals more tears to fall. "I will be like Prometheus, and Ireneus, men who never brought harm to anyone!" I finally admit, collapsing to my knees as hot tears flood my eyes and burn my face with fear.

"If you are truly a Soukina, then you shouldn't feel guilty about what happened to Ireneus. Just as Diokles won't shed a single tear over the loss of one of his most trusted and loyal soldiers, a man who died a senseless death because his leader covets men's respect to the point of obsession."

"Diokles understands the value of sacrifice," I say, but the sentence feels foreign on my tongue; I quickly realize I am quoting Alexa's words to me as we rode through the desert on the back of the Centaur, when she reproved me for not risking death to kill Acheron. To her, and the rest of her brother's army, an unfinished task is far better than a task left untried.

"A high price must be paid if we ever want to be free from the Alphas," I say, wiping my tears and crawling into a narrow net of shade being cast from the wall. "I don't deny that it is often hard to accept, but – "

"Iris," Tycho says softly. "Do you really believe that a thousand angry Eusebians can so much as puncture a hole in the armor of the Alphas?"

"You did," I answer, my curiosity piquing. "What happened to you?"

Tycho takes a deep breath and rakes his fingers through his hair.

"I wish I had time to tell you," he says. "But we aren't safe here."

"*You* aren't safe here," I correct him. "I will tell Diokles that you've killed his man and deserted us, that I found the body but you were already gone."

Clap... Clap... Clap...

Tycho and I spin around like startled sheep to face whatever wolf has cornered us. There, looming over me, with a hand on his sword and a smile on his lips, is the general Titus.

"A clever plan, young Soukina," he says to me. "If only it would work..."

Watching my red, tear-stung eyes fill up again, he turns his attention to Tycho.

"Tycho, good to see you, old friend!"

If I didn't know better, I'd think him genuinely pleased to see his conscripted comrade.

"I regret that I missed your induction this morning. I was pleased to hear that you've lived to see another day," says Titus.

"And you," Tycho says, extending his hand.

Titus removes his hand from his sword and shakes Tycho's hand.

"Poor Patroclus," he says, regarding the dead soldier.

Then he looks at me with a loud sigh, like a father ready to chide his recalcitrant child. But he doesn't ask me anything.

"Go, Tycho. The young Soukina will stay with me now."

Tycho walks over to me and lifts me to my feet and lightly pulls me out of the shadow. He places my hair behind my ear and whispers into it, "You will be all right."

Though there is no breeze, I feel chills rising on the back of my neck. My mouth opens, my lips begin to move, but my mind is void of a response.

"Trust me."

With those words, Tycho squeezes my hand, brings his cloak over his head, and begins his escape from Ēlektōr.

And suddenly, I have words to say, my first prayer since the day my brother died:

"Duna, please...watch over him."

CHAPTER EIGHTEEN
EXECUTIONER

I feel strangely subdued as Titus turns my shoulders to the north and leads me in silence toward the summit's gates. Surely Tycho would not save my life twice only to leave it in enemy hands...

What do you know, Tycho? What makes you trust the general?

"Trust me," is the fruitless reply I receive again and again as I mull over the few things I've learned about Tycho and Titus, two men who have shown me inexplicable kindness amid a people who consider such a virtue to be anathema, a deplorable stain in the fabric of their uniquely Soukinoi ideals.

Tycho was once a Pythonian servant, and once a valuable Soukinoi soldier. Now, it is made plain by his constant prayers and a baffling concern for me, a bullheaded, blood-spilling orphan, that he is an unabashed follower of Duna, and one who has come to view a Eusebian revolt of vengeance and terror as a sinful, and indeed a futile enterprise.

It is much more difficult trying to decipher exactly where Titus's loyalty lies.

The enigmatic eyes of the general couldn't stop my soul from feeling an unexplainable connection to his own the moment I met him. His advice to me in the tavern to eat as much breakfast as I could seemed a cryptic allusion to my forthcoming mission. And his last words to me, "you'll find that Soukinoi life is a continuous stream of surprises," were perhaps the most mysterious of all.

"You're making me suspicious, Soukina," Titus says as we begin our descent down the mountain.

Just then, the Gryphon begins her wailing demand for supper, and I am happy to be distracted by an opportunity for conversation.

"I'm making *you* suspicious?" I ask with a laugh. Has it not crossed his mind that it's quite possible I have found *his* actions of late to be a bit peculiar?

"You've been following me, docile as a pony, for nearly an hour and haven't whinnied a word," he says, turning and looking at me with a charming half smile.

"I know better than to be anything *but* docile, sir," I say. "You needn't be suspicious. You can even confiscate my dagger if it would make you feel better."

I smile as I unsheathe my knife and hold it out for him to take. He laughs and waves it away, then goes totally still, his face and body appearing so pallid and frozen that I wonder if he will faint.

"Are you all right?" I ask, sheathing my dagger and stepping slowly toward him.

Titus takes a step backwards off the path and crouches there, holding a hand to his heart as rays of setting sun pour color back into his face.

Then, with his other hand he reaches into his belt and pulls something out of it, but promptly forms a tight fist to conceal whatever it holds.

A knife? Hemlock?

"What? Am I to die here? Right now? ... Tell me!" I implore.

"No, Iris. Listen to me..." he says calmly, standing back up again. "This is all very new to me; I haven't been quite sure how to handle it. And now, it's affecting my health!"

"Handle what?" I ask.

"Let's keep moving. Idleness will only draw attention."

I follow as Titus continues leading us down the mountain, lifting his chin and nodding curtly to a pair of soldiers, each riding a stolen Alpha stallion up to its new home.

"I had a dream a few days ago after my prayers in the temple. Actually, I don't remember ever falling asleep...all of it seemed so real...Have you ever had a dream like that?" he asks me.

"A dream, no. A nightmare, yes," I reply, anxious to reach the end of his revelation.

"I was by myself in the cella when it happened. I saw a bright flash of light, and then a girl appeared in the midst of it. I thought at first it was Alexa, but when the light faded away, I saw it couldn't be. This girl had auburn hair, and splendid robes that were –"

"Deep blue, like the sea," I say, not the slightest bit surprised. I look around the barren slope to see if the elusive messenger is here now, waiting for me with another riddle to sing or a stone to give. But all I see are Diokles's men below, scurrying about his makeshift palace like rats around a nest.

"Yes. So you do know her! You do know Carya! I haven't lost my mind!" he exclaims, almost bounding forward in his relief. But he swiftly contains himself and lowers his voice to whisper, "I thought it was a dream, but she gave me something." He looks down at his fist. "I still have it."

I reach into the pouch around my waist and pull out my own gift from Carya.

"I presume she has a message for me," I say, rubbing the jasper stone between my fingers, waiting for the right moment to bring it into the light and corroborate his encounter.

Titus scratches his head. "Yes...but, like I said, this is – this is extraordinary!" He says, tilting his head toward me and talking from one side of his mouth. "Everything she told me would happen *has happened*." He pauses as an actor would to ensure he's got the audience's attention. "First she told me Tycho had been captured by Soukinoi in Limén. Then she said that during his final mission as a Soukinos, he had saved the life of the girl I found in the desert – you, of course – and that I should give you a message if you intervened for him the day he was returned here to Ēlektōr. And you did."

Titus stops on the path and turns to me, anticipating a question, or a gasp of disbelief, but I keep walking, kicking pebbles as I go along, and contentedly breathing in lungs-full of cool evening air.

"She must be a goddess, this Carya," Titus starts again, thirsty for discussion. "But there is no such thing. That much I know."

I smile a little at the mystified general. Never would anyone suspect that he, a stalwart, flinty, and unflappable soldier, was at this moment seeking religious insight from a mildly educated orphan recruit.

"Is something funny, Soukina?" he asks. I shake my head and press my lips together, erasing my smile.

"No, sir. It's just – well, never mind. Carya is a nymph," I say, getting back to the subject at hand.

"A nymph!" he repeats, as though he misheard me. "Like the berserk ones in the Alphas' stories, draped in fawn skins and running around the woods with pine-cone staffs? The ones who raised Dionysus in a cave before he grew up and became a god of wine and abject debauchery?" He chuckles, "Carya is one of those?"

I realize I'd never thought it through. All this time, I've been blinded to the stark contradictions surrounding my ideas of Carya's identity. Since the day I met her in the moonlight near my mother's death bed, I have called her "nymph." But according to Eusebian prophecy, such creatures are, at best, nothing more than imaginary froth, and at worst, harmful distractions, inconspicuous diversions from the one true, unequaled god...

"I don't know," I confess. "I suppose I don't know what else she could be."

"Call her a messenger," Titus says, employing his authoritative tone. "We demean Duna's servants by likening them to maniacal pagan shrews."

"Fair enough," I say, respectful of the man's convictions. "Now can you relay the...*messenger's* message?" I remember to add, "Please, general?"

"The hour I prayed for a clear sense of Duna's vision for my life here, my purpose here, I'm given a visitation with a goddess – er, a messenger – that I cannot deny, and that you have confirmed! Forgive me, but my mind is rather muddled, Soukina. I never thought our Creator would insinuate himself into a soldier's affairs, least of all mine."

"Please, Just try," I urge him, ignoring his sentiment. "You don't have to remember every word."

The general sighs loudly and slows his pace, thinking silently and then mumbling unintelligibly over Carya's rhymes. And then confident, crisp, coherent words come forth:

"Below amber lies the emerald arc among the Moonbow's hues,
A color of life, a stone of growth, a new beginning if you choose,
Forgive and be forgiven, take the green gem held nearby,
In the hand of the one who held the torch, and watched your brother die."

A few long moments pass as the message sinks into my skin, slips into my veins, and circulates through my body like a virus until it reaches my heart, gripping it, twisting it as I do the same to the hilt of my dagger. Maybe this time I will have the courage to use it.

"*You* killed my brother?!" I scream, not caring who might hear. Titus doesn't try to quiet me, but sadly hangs his head as though a heavy yoke were around his neck.

"It seems you and I worked for the same man," he says.

"*Acheron...*" I spit the name from my mouth like a poison.

"He offered me more wealth than I have ever known to be his bodyguard, promised me my family would always be safe as long as I kept *him* safe." Titus begins walking again as his memories wash over him. "One night while he was away, his house was burned to the ground, by arsonists or accident, no one knows. The next night..." he stops and gazes out at the peach-colored clouds painted across the horizon. "My wife and two sons were killed, tied to their beds and burned alive. From then on, I was Acheron's executioner, made to listen and watch as men, women, and countless innocents were consumed with fire..."

Titus turns away from me, his shoulders heaving up and down as he cries to himself in silence.

I wait for the swell of wrath to rise up in me at any second, for lava-hot anger to send me running toward the executioner and stabbing him a hundred times – no doma needed. How I have waited for this moment! How I have longed to seize revenge like a jewel-encrusted chalice and fill it until it overflows with the blood of all who destroyed my life and oppress my people. But now that the moment is here, I am overcome not with rage, but with empathy.

"Perhaps I should have taken your dagger when I had the chance," says Titus, mustering a laugh as he eyes the weapon in my hand.

Titus goes to his knees, surrenders his sword on the ground in front of me, and lowers his head, ready to receive whatever blow I have in mind for it.

"I won't defend against it. I deserve justice," he says. "My only request... Make it quick."

CHAPTER NINETEEN
EMERALD

G eneral," I whisper, half baffled, half relieved that I cannot kill him. "When did you leave?"

He looks up at me with surprise.

"Pardon me?" he says.

"When did you leave Acheron? And stand up, sir. I can't do this," I add, sheathing my knife and pushing his sword back toward him with my sandal. Somehow, the desire to kill, to *avenge*, has been summarily dissolved, replaced by unexpected feelings of pity, sorrow, and of kinship for the general.

"Your mercy will not be forgotten," he says, rising and taking his sword. "You are truly your brother's sister."

"You didn't know my brother!" I retort, my skin prickling instantly with indignation, but the temperature of my blood doesn't shift.

"I left Acheron the morning following your brother's death. I'd heard him and the others of the Hodos who died that night speak in the streets on several occasions," he says somberly. "They spoke of Phos, the Light of Petros, and the peace he gives to anyone who believes that he is who he said he was, and that he died for us. Diokles was looking for more recruits. And I was looking for a purpose. Much like yourself."

"Phos didn't give my brother – or his friends – any *peace*!" I say, bitterness burning and closing around my throat. "He brought them to Enochos and stood back as they suffered. And you have no idea what I'm looking for!"

I spot an Acacia tree to my right and walk briskly to it, eager to rest my feet and steal a moment of solitude. Titus kindly keeps his distance as I collect a handful of seeds and store them up for later. I remove the jasper stone from my girdle, kiss it and clasp it tight as I lean my head against the tree and gaze at the rising moon peering over the desert, a lustrous pupil within a silken socket of clouds.

And then I think of Carya's song to Titus: "*The green gem that is near...*"

"General!" I call. He turns to me and I wait for him to come closer.

"Soukina, we should go now. Diokles is expecting me," he says.

"Expecting *us,* you mean."

Titus doesn't have an answer to give, no reassuring words or even a well-crafted lie to offer. He only stares at the ethereal eye as it shines the beneficent light of heaven over our darkness.

"I know that you must deliver me to him," I say as I stand, noticing the fresh, redolent smell of rain wafting down from a dense caravan of clouds hanging low above our heads. "And I still don't want to kill you." I grasp Titus's shoulder, and as he looks in my eyes, I know that he believes I mean it.

"You can trust me, Soukina."

"That's what Tycho said," I say as my mind dispatches another prayer for my friend. "He hasn't betrayed me yet."

The clouds release a few sprinkles of rain, each tiny splash on my forehead admonishing me to continue walking before the imminent downpour...or perhaps before Diokles suspects that his general is now following the orders of a nymph-like servant of Duna.

"Now I *trust* you to tell me more about the green gem you've got in your hand," I smile.

"That's right," remembers Titus. "So this means you have forgiven me, then?"

"Excuse me?" I ask.

"Carya said the gem becomes yours if you forgive me for what I did at Enochos."

I answer only with a deep breath and a silent curse. *What does forgiveness have to do with anything?*

"I would pay any price to undo all the wrong I've done, Iris. I would give my own life. I am sorry," he pleads, the words spilling hastily into the air as though they'd been trapped for lightless ages, left suffocating inside his soul.

Forgiveness. The last person I forgave was my own mother just a few days before her spirit left this world, driven away by the fever that had taken my father from us.

She had emerged from her delirium, her cough and chills had subsided, even the rosy rash on her chest appeared fainter. She asked Jasper to carry her up onto the roof to enjoy the sunshine one last time. No sooner had we gone up than her coughing returned. But she refused to be taken inside.

"I'm not dead yet!" she said. "I feel like I'm lying halfway inside my tomb while in that room."

So Jasper and I reclined alongside her and welcomed the sound and sight of any bird or breeze or butterfly that could brighten the shroud of death that was draped over us.

When a friendly moth with dusky white wings alighted on her shoulder, I said with the cheeriest tone I could muster, "Those are drawn to the light, mother. Maybe it's a sign that you're going to be well!"

She reached over to me, took my hand, and after a brief coughing spell replied, "Or maybe it will help draw *me* to the light..." She smiled as the moth took flight once again toward the tops of the poplar trees, fading like a ghost as it climbed on toward the sun. "When the time is right," she added, kissing my cheek.

"I miss you!" I cried out, my hopeful countenance evaporating at the thought of her spirit following the path of the moth.

"She's right here with you, Iris," Jasper said, watching as she pulled me onto her lap, her baby girl again.

Then why does she seem so far away? I remember thinking, as I wrapped my arms around her neck and buried my face in her hair, hoping that if I wished hard enough I could send us back in time, back to when I *was* a baby and the world was just beginning...

"I want to ask something of you both," she said.

"Anything, mother," Jasper replied, walking over to sit at our feet.

"I ask that you would forgive me."

"Mother, what on earth for?" Jasper asked, his face blanched with bewilderment.

"For not being here to watch you both grow up. For not being here to see you as a beautiful bride, Iris, a mother, a great explorer like you've always wanted to be. For not being here to see you become the leader and teacher Duna has called you to be, Jasper. I pray that he lets me see pieces from above. Who knows, maybe there's a cloud with my name on it, where I can lie and look down on you both any hour of the day!" she said as I crawled off her lap and cried as silently as I could.

"Oh Iris, don't be sad," she said. "I'm going to see your father soon, and I know you'll have lots of hugs and kisses for me to deliver to him, isn't that right?" Reluctantly, I nod my head and find solace in the daydream of my mother and father united again in a utopia free of fevers and tears and lives cut short.

"That means you have forgiven me, then?" she asked, just as Titus has today.

Jasper and I shouted an enthusiastic "Yes!" in unison, and together we sat on the roof until dark, forgoing sleep and supper to stretch out the day, to freeze time, if it were possible. And at her insistent request, we described for our mother every detail of the dreams we had for ourselves, dreams none of us could have imagined would be snuffed out by death, slavery, and a desert of rebellion.

A blue bolt of lightning flashing over the mountain brings my attention back to the man asking for my forgiveness.

"I could lie you know," I say with a smirk. "I could tell you that I forgive you just so I can have the stone." But I am fooling no one. The relief I observed on my mother's face when Jasper and I released her of the burden of guilt she bore impressed me greater than I ever realized. I learned that forgiveness is a finespun sort of phenomenon, possessing a quality I can only describe as magical. I felt that as I gave it to my mother, I was receiving for myself something equally precious.

"You could," concedes Titus. "And you would have no one but Duna to judge you for it." He gives me a wink, but I know there is a warning in his words.

"I should – I should be angry," I stammer, my feelings of frustration hindering my tongue just as it has my logic throughout this tedious trek down the mountain.

Forgive the man who killed your brother? How foolish can you be!

"The only reason I am in this forsaken place is because I know that Diokles will lead me to Acheron and set our people free," I say, speaking the words like a dispassionate orator reading from a scroll. "And here you are, the man who set fire to Jasper's pyre; I should be ecstatic!" The words come out effortlessly now. "Why can't I kill you? What don't I feel one iota of anger when I look at you?! I forgive you, general."

And I feel it. Forgiveness enchanting me, calming me, cleansing me. I force one foot in front of the other as the wind blows, carrying in the storm from the distant sea.

"Soukina," he says, following after me. "You love your brother, don't you."

"More than anything."

"When my wife and sons were alive, I lived to love them, protect them, and make them proud. There were many times I walked away from battles and laid aside offenses simply because I knew it pleased them, because it is what they wanted. Do you understand?"

I nod, knowing undoubtedly that Jasper would be proud that I have let forgiveness win. My brother gave the clothes off his back, the meat from his table to anyone in need of it. After he devoted himself to the Hodos, he was routinely mocked, ostracized, and imprisoned for his beliefs, but never once did he speak of vengeance or utter a single syllable of complaint; rather, he *rejoiced* in his sufferings. "I give thanks that I have been found worthy to suffer disgrace for the name of Phos," he'd say.

It was when I heard him speak words so incomprehensible, so absurd-sounding as those that I questioned whether he or I was adopted. On the nights I was whipped by Acheron, or given only crumbs off his plate for supper, my mind alternated between dreaming of life with my family on the limestone cliffs, and longing to be sucked into the Styx and released from my misery. I had nothing to smile or sing about, and giving thanks was done only out of fear and compulsion when Acheron pointed to emaciated beggars on the street and demanded of Niobe and me, "Are you not grateful that I have saved you from such a fate?"

"I can see Jasper smiling now," I say to Titus. "But I think there is more to my *tolerance* of you than you realize," I say.

"And what is that?" he replies, his eyebrow lifting with curiosity.

BOOM!

The patience of the storm has run out. Thunder rolls across the sky, covering the moon and saturating everything below it in a pale, green, gossamery tint. The light rain that had been for us a refreshing mist transforms into a torrent of icy water and relentless wind that sends us retreating down the path to the temple where Diokles is waiting.

As we pick up our pace, I feel Titus place in my hand what can be none other than the green gem. I cannot wait; I stop only for a moment and carefully open up my palm to get a peek of Carya's promise to me: a perfect emerald oval, no larger than a pomegranate seed, and filled with a brilliance that, indeed, I've only beheld in the Moonbow's arches.

I secure the emerald in my pouch along with my jasper stone, one a token of forgiveness and flourishing life, the other a symbol of strength for storms, both above and within, and of hope for the breaking day.

CHAPTER TWENTY
APOLLO

We make it to the temple, out of breath from the storm's fierce chase. The sentries at the steps salute their general and direct us toward the cella, its door cracked open allowing the spicy smell of laurel incense to drift out of the blackness.

I follow Titus into the room and make out Diokles's silhouette lying supine on the floor. His fingers are spread wide, the whites of his eyes almost aglow in the dark as his lips move soundlessly and his body jerks in startling convulsions. I nudge the general's side.

"What's happening?" I whisper. Titus doesn't answer me, but steps toward Diokles.

"Diokles," he says. "It's General Titus with the young Soukina."

Diokles doesn't respond but continues to writhe like a man underfoot of the Minotaur.

"A...poll...o..." Diokles groans in a fearsome voice, his arms and legs flailing in all directions. "Speak to your oracle..."

Diokles's body goes rigid. His lips tighten and eyes close as he takes a big breath through his nostrils and exhales with a horrifying wail that seems to make the lamplight grow dim with fear as all warmth escapes the room.

I feel Titus's lean into me as he turns to leave. I follow him out, shutting the door securely behind me.

"What was that about?" I ask Titus as we make our way a safe distance from the cella onto the portico.

"Believe me when I tell you, I have never witnessed such – such insanity," he says, shaking his head, evidently ashamed of his leader's frenzy.

"He said *'Apollo'*," I think aloud. "An Alpha deity, god of prophecy, healing, and the sun. Eusebians pray to Duna alone."

"How do you know so much about the pagan gods?" asks Titus, trying hard to conceal his suspicion.

"Acheron had many scrolls. And I had many idle hours while he was away," I confess, remembering the long summer afternoons I sat beneath a myrtle tree, sacred to Aphrodite, and read and read again the myths of the conniving gods and the heroes of old with whom they meddled and spawned the *hemitheoi,* half-gods, like ravishing Helen and matchless Heracles.

Had Acheron kept in his library a single Eusebian scroll about the true Creator and the patriarchs of our faith, I would have read it a thousand times instead of filling my head with pagan filth and heresies, a pastime that would have earned me thirty days in the tannery kneading dung-soaked animal skins with my bare feet.

The longer I learned about the wars, the affairs, the murders and lies of the Alpha pantheon, the more I wondered if such evil truly was the product of men's imaginations, fantasies no more real than the disjointed dreams and dreadful chimeras that disappear when light hits our eyes.

What kind of mind could conceive of these atrocities? I'd asked myself.

Apollo, the lyre-plucking god of music and a friend to swans and dolphins, was also a vindictive murderer whose bow slayed innocent children and whose pride hung a musician of lesser skill from the limb of a lofty pine, flayed him, and let him dangle until dead.

In another story, Apollo tried to seduce the princess Cassandra. As a youth, the maiden and her brother spent a night in his temple. As they slumbered, enchanted serpents of the god entwined themselves with the children and used their wily tongues to flick the gift of soothsaying into their ears. Years later, she visited the temple again. But this night, she was not met by magical creatures but by their master, the destroyer-god himself. Apollo tried to seduce the nubile princess, but she refused him, provoking the wrathful deity to curse her prophecies so that no one would ever believe them, a curse that led ultimately to her murder at the hands of a jealous queen.

How could anyone love this god enough to find him worthy of offering bloody sacrifices and throwing men from rocks for the god's good pleasure? How could Alphas worship a god who makes sport of tormenting helpless mortals?

But it occurs to me... Apollo and the other gods were never loved – they were feared. There was a time when a man or woman would do anything to appease or win favor with the gods, even let their newborn infant burn within the belly of a brazen bull while they drowned out its screams with drums and dancing.

The recurring question of whether it was merely gifted storytellers – with nothing more than human experience to inspire them – who invented the grisly Alpha myths and the abominable rituals of their religion continues to itch at the back of my mind. Maybe Diokles has the answers I'm looking for...

"You did not take me by surprise, my friends."

Titus and I glance at one another and slowly turn toward the cella from whence the honeyed words ooze toward us. In the midst of the portico stands

Diokles, sparkling white from head to toe, magnific as a marble statue. Even his wavy locks are light as ocean foam, but his eyes are still cerulean as they ever were, the striking color of the sea below a sky indwelled by the sun god...

"Apollo," I whisper to myself.

"Apollo, you say?" asks Diokles, a hand cupping his ear as he takes a few steps forward. "You are correct. But I am not the god. I – " He quickly pivots around and back again, surveying the portico for any guards, then grins at us like a misbehaving child gloating in his defiance. "Come with me. I will tell you everything."

<hr/>

I feel I have no other choice but to follow the general as he obeys his would-be emperor. We return in silence to the cella, and I try hard to suppress the visions of serpents and the hissing sound my mind insists is flowing from the lamps around the room.

Those are only made-up myths, Iris. Not one word of them is real, I tell myself.

"Come. Sit with me," says Diokles, his tone uncharacteristically calm, his manner unusually relaxed.

We follow him to the front of the cramped, cave-like room near the niche that houses the sacred scrolls. I sit down, stretch out my legs, and lean back with a deep breath, feeling so at ease that even the sudden drop in temperature lends itself to my restful state as I stare at the godlike leader and marvel at a glistening light, like a living fire, dancing across his marble skin. My eyes move slowly over to Titus who stands at attention against the wall.

"Good general," says Diokles. "Do make yourself comfortable. There are guards outside, and... we're in the middle of a desert!" he laughs. "Let's not be silly!" I join him in laughter until Titus finally sheds his soldierly demeanor and takes a seat on the cold stone floor. But he doesn't crack a smile.

"You know something of Apollo, do you, Iris?" Diokles asks nonchalantly.

"Only a little," I reply, looking around the room for the source of the strong laurel scent, but I see no reflective sheen of an altar. "I know that the laurel tree is a symbol of Apollo, consecrated by him after one of the maidens he pursued became one, just to escape him."

"Yes. And the spattering of Apollonian worshippers that are left still burn its leaves as offerings to him," Diokles adds. "General, do you smell the laurel fragrance of which I am sure the Soukina is reminded?"

Titus nods, "Yes, sir."

"And do you think that *I*, your Eusebian brother and sworn rebel against the Alpha tyrants, am one of his worshippers?"

"I couldn't say, sir."

"You couldn't say." Diokles gives a condescending smirk. "But I suppose I too would be sitting there emulating the manner of a stupefied eunuch if I were as unenlightened as the rest of you." Diokles turns to me with an apologetic, downward tilt of his chin. "Soukina, forgive me – *you* are a rarity. Your knowledge will make the truth much easier to accept."

Diokles stands up and walks in front of the niche. His statue-like skin regains its normal, olive complexion as he bends down and reaches into the niche, pulling out an amber tablet.

"The hallowed scrolls," he says, "have their place. But they are just threads, just a small, almost imperceptible segment of wisdom within a tapestry much grander than I ever imagined!"

I lean forward and sit cross-legged like an enraptured child, intrigued beyond measure to hear more of this mystery, to learn of the things which have been hidden from me, and perhaps from everyone who has been too distracted to notice, or too prideful to learn.

"Do you want to know more?" asks Diokles, taunting me.

"Yes sir!" I reply without hesitation.

"Sir, I should leave. I have training to – " begins Titus.

"You will stay!" Diokles barks. "It is time you heard the revelation, general. I will need military men of your caliber to also have at least an elementary grasp of what and who we're really fighting for."

"*Who,* sir?" Titus asks.

"So you *do* want to know," smiles Diokles. Titus remains seated, but cracks his knuckles nervously until a deep breath calms him down.

Why is he being so odd? I think. But I feel too content, too disconnected from any care to concern my thoughts with him for more than a moment.

Why are you *being so odd?* An inner voice asks. Again, I don't pay the words any mind but keep my wide eyes fixed on Diokles.

"I am Eusebian as each of you are. But we can also be more, much, much more," Diokles begins again. "The Alphas are no more special, no more favored by the gods than we. But they were, at one time, the recipients of esoteric knowledge – because their eyes were opened, their spirits attuned to the will of watching immortals."

"So the myths are true?" I ask.

"Their origins are true. And that is all that matters. There is a grain of truth in every myth, but their intended function is to forever remind us of what's always been around us: powerful entities with the ability to help us ascend to greater heights and achieve our full potential, or to destroy us should we resist."

"And Python, then?" Titus asks. "Does he serve himself, or Apollo?"

"Apollo and Python are one," Diokles says coolly, as though the answer was obvious.

"Then he is an enemy of Duna, sir. We cannot serve him!" asserts Titus as he stands in protest.

"Shhh...Calm down, general. I was once groping about the darkness like yourself. I was skeptical, too, the first time Apollo appeared to me in this cella." A blinding flash of light shoots across Diokles's skin. "But he has made all things clear to me."

Diokles's voice is low, peaceful, free, welcoming as the ocean waves that lapped the cliffs beneath my home in Eirene.

"Please tell us more, Diokles. What things did the god tell you?" I ask.

Diokles smiles, turning his back to us. "I would like to tell you, sister. And perhaps I shall. But we mustn't get ahead of ourselves." He stands idle for a moment, then violently stretches his arms wide like Gryphon wings and spins around with a beastly snarl.

Titus and I watch as Diokles's blithesome expression melts from his face like cocky Icarus's waxen wings when he flew too near the sun. His golden eyebrows narrow. A swarm of shadows creeps out from the walls and begins to brood over his face, sucking the color from his eyes and replacing them with wide black spheres of onyx. He whips his head toward Titus like an owl who's spotted a mouse, then points a finger at me.

"First, young Soukina, we have a bit of business to discuss," Diokles says, his voice deep and cavernous. "General, tell me where you found our brave young warrior. Was she with her friend?"

"Sir? Her friend?" Titus's feigned confusion even convinces me that he is unsure what his master means.

"Come now, general. Was she with the one for whom she so *courageously* risked her life? The one for whom she *continues* to risk her life?"

"With Tycho, sir?" Titus says, sounding only a little less muddled. "Yes, sir. I found her at the southern wall just after – "

"I care not for any wearisome details, general. I know that the traitor killed Patroclus. He was no match for Tycho. And now he will be stoned as I said he would be, and the girl will be in the Gryphon's jaws by sunrise. Speaking of the Gryphon..." Diokles presses both forefingers contemplatively to his lips and faces the wall. "Did you know she has a name?"

"No, sir," I reply.

"She has a very beautiful name, one fit for an Asher like yourself. *Corinna...* Perhaps you know it?"

Corinna. My mother's sister who went missing when she was just a little girl.

It's impossible... Isn't it?

The silence is deafening. The eerie, dreamlike peace I've been immersed in sinks into the floor and recedes into the roof, leaving me wide awake, trapped inside a wolf's den. I feel the color drain from my face, my heart beating fast, pumping fire through my veins.

"What have you done to my aunt?!" I try to yell, but my lungs feel weak. All my energy is concentrated on forcing the doma to work. It must work!

"Iris, don't overreact," Diokles says, still turned away. "I see you clenching those unruly fists of yours. I only granted her wishes, helped her master her wings and learn to fly. Well you know this – you've experienced it! Quite a gift, isn't it? Apollo was gracious in bestowing to her a form better suited to her disposition." He turns to me with a nauseous smile.

"She does more than fly, sir. She's a killer," says Titus, his jaw set, his voice oscillating between tones of rage and sadness.

"She was always a killer, general. She'd been a vagabond for decades, killing for food, for self-preservation... Her whole life had been spent fleeing from Pythonians who sought to sacrifice her for their own selfish gain. But Apollo had greater plans for her, and he entrusted me with the task of helping her realize them. And now she is unrecognizable to the other, *misguided* Pythonians. Those without the vision for the coming age."

"Selfish gain..." I growl. "And what you've done to her, turning her into a monster, stealing her humanity and keeping her locked inside a cage, is not for your profit?" My arms sting with the surge of fire. My palms start to tremble as they secrete tiny yellow bubbles of heat. "What you would do to me you would do *expressly* for your selfish gain!"

Feeling the fire boil, ready to unseal my skin and send flames speeding toward their target, I raise my hands toward Diokles, but they immediately collapse back down to my thighs under the weight of an invisible force, a freezing gust of wind that causes my sweat to crystallize and my fingertips to shrivel and darken till they appear as wizened grapes hanging dead at the ends of my hands.

"What are you doing?" I cry out, my breath like smoke in the numinous wall of winter around me.

"I am sorry, Soukina. I wanted to teach you about your doma, as I taught Corinna about hers. I wanted you to have the pleasure of killing Acheron in Eirene. But, I'm afraid you will not receive the truth, or the vengeance, you are seeking. Alexa will be very disappointed. You showed such promise..." Diokles turns back to Titus. "The traitor is in the prison?"

Speak, Titus! my head screams, causing my temples to throb.

"Tycho escaped," Titus says, rushing to my side as I fall to the floor, shaking and coughing as I did the night I was pulled from icy Enochos by Acheron, a man whose evil I once thought unsurpassed.

"And no one has gone after him?!" Diokles yells, his eyes completely overcome with smoldering blackness.

"No one was with me. I can dispatch the psiloi now. Just don't hurt the gir – "

"There will be no need to dispatch them now, general. Time is up."

Diokles steps out of the room and leaves the door open, the warm, fresh air and bright light too tempting to resist...

My body finally thawing, I break away from Titus before he can say a word, and follow Diokles out the door. I tiptoe as quietly as I can in the opposite direction, then start to run across the portico, faster and faster, wishing my doma would manifest, that wings would sprout from my shoulder blades, or that heroic Pegasus would swoop down from the clouds and carry me back to Limén, back to Gennadius and Aspasia.

But I have no such fortune. Waiting for me at the edge of the temple are six armed guards on horseback, with nothing but sheets of rain and not one shred of hope between us.

CHAPTER TWENTY-ONE
ESCAPE

I didn't struggle as they arrested me and bound my hands behind my back. I didn't scream as they began pulling me along behind them with a rope around my neck like an animal headed to slaughter. I didn't cry out for Titus to rescue me or for Diokles to have mercy.

All the way to the Soukinoi prison, my eyes were transfixed by the Moonbow, barely distinguishable within the dampened light of the moon; I doubt the others even noticed it. But I did, because it, or more likely its creator, has proven worthy of searching for in the vast expanse of heaven. Since I first witnessed it at my mother's death, it has been a constant shadow, a silent companion, one I chose for so long to denigrate and ignore. I see now that it is no shadow at all, but a reflection of something true, something eternal, something Jasper understood and prayed for me to embrace as well.

Held aloft in the dark chamber of night by a phantasmal web of wispy clouds and timid stars, the Moonbow, too, seemed trapped in a prison cell. Every arch, from the scarlet first to the violet seventh, appeared pale and oddly distant from one another, almost as if they were being pulled apart, unwelcomed by this oppressive sector of Petrodian sky stretching over Ēlektōr. But seeing it there, even if it seemed but a ghost of its usual form, was an ineffable comfort to me. And as I was dragged into the rose-colored cave and made to watch as Titus was flogged and beaten until his eyes swelled shut and the sandstone walls around us were covered in his blood, I clung to the jasper and emerald stones and whispered another prayer:

"Duna, if it is possible, spare us from dying here. And let me make it to Therismos. Let me kill Acheron."

❦

I finally put the stone back into the pouch and welcome a light westerly wind greeting me from the mountaintop, hoping it will coax my eyes to close and my restless mind to dream. But I cannot sleep. How can I when all around me is the sight of spattered blood, the sound of Titus's moaning, and the noxious smell of –

"I had a feeling you'd be joining me."

The low voice rises out of its cell like a miasmic vapor. As it itches my ears, I see the speaker's shadow, which comprises a man's head and torso, but the body and hooves of a horse.

"Centaur...?" I whisper.

"What gave it away?" he snorts, pawing the floor and swishing his tail.

"I had a feeling you'd be dead," I said, wrapping my hands around the iron bars and looking to my left, then to my right where a guard sleeps against the wall, a bronze key hanging from his neck.

"Diokles told them not to harm me," he says.

152

"Why not?"

"I've been trying to figure that out since the day that yellow-haired urchin had me locked up in here," he says, then steps into the moonlight, his chestnut coat just as filthy and his face just as hideous as I remember. "And I think I've come up with the answer," he says.

"Oh yes? And what answer is that?"

"I'm simply far too beautiful to kill," he answers with the ugliest crooked grin I've ever seen. "Centaurs are nearly an extinct species. Diokles rightly won't stand for a creature as rare and exquisite as I to perish."

"I think you are absolutely correct, Centaur," I laugh, stopping only when the sleeping guard rouses and in a sleepy stupor barks:

"Quiet! Or I'll cut off your ears!"

The Centaur winks at me and tugs on his ears, and I return to my mat on the floor and pray once more for the impossible.

⚬⚬⚬

I must be dreaming. My surroundings are the same, and Titus still groans, but the smell of the air is different. While it had once been polluted with the Centaur's stench and the metallic scent of blood, it is now infused with the smells of lilac and citrus, sweet harbingers of spring. The moon is gone, sunken into the crepuscular sea of twilight, and yet I make out a faint blue halo of light just outside the cave walls that intensifies with every inch it draws nearer.

"Prayer is the thread that never breaks,
Blue is the form that your answer takes.
It is time to leave this desert of schemes,
And the man bewitched by vile dreams.
Go into Eirene when these bars are broken;
The command of Duna has been spoken."

I know without question it is Carya who sings and animates this brilliant blue orb; I can almost see her auburn hair and crown of pearls shining within it like waves transformed by the sunset.

The tinging sound of a sword being pulled from its scabbard shakes Titus awake. He raises both fists as he stumbles to his feet and tries to look around the cell, but his eyes are blinded by welts and purple bruises.

"Iris?!" he shouts. "Are you here?!"

"I'm here!" I reply in a whisper. "Be quiet!"

I rush to the bars and breathe a sigh of relief when I find the guard is somehow still asleep. Turning back around, I see the blue halo forming itself, from top to bottom, into the leaf-shaped blade of a sword. It floats slowly through the spring-smelling air and stops before the prison bars where it begins to pulsate with spectacular beams of light, the colors of which I've never seen before.

Carya's invisible hand positions the sword's glowing tip on the center bar and drags it across the row of iron, sending silent sparks of blue and white into the air like a bouquet of exploding stardust.

The Centaur approaches his bars just as the sword starts to fade into a hazy afterglow and mouths the words, "What was that?"

He and Titus sit down, but I remain standing, keeping my eyes steady on the bars where I discern a clean, minuscule line bisecting each one.

Now what, Carya? I think.

And then something compels me to grab hold of two bars, just below the perfectly straight line sliced across them. The Centaur cocks his head at my peculiar conduct, which he probably thinks a rather feeble attempt at escape.

"Shh! Shh!" I say.

But it's too late. The guard's eyes flash open and the phantom sword vanishes before touching the final bar.

I pull on the bars in my hand as hard as I can, but am thrown backwards by the force of my effort. My jaw drops at the sight of the two iron bars resting on the ground in front of me.

"Well that was a neat trick, whatever that was!" the Centaur says. "Aren't you the lucky one!"

I close my eyes and pray for one more "trick." Then, faster than I can think, I lift a flickering hand to the Centaur's cell and watch as a spray of flames glitters its course across the bars, causing the beast to buck and whinny with fright.

"Settle down, Centaur!" Then I make a pulling motion with both hands and watch as the wisps of smoke wafting out of them mingle with the blue, left-over light of Carya's sword, forming a vaporous mural as it eddies upward into the cold, dank air.

The Centaur obeys my mimed command and tugs on one bar, only slightly, sending it to the ground as though it were nothing more than flaxen thread unraveling from a spool.

"What sorcery!" he exclaims, kicking up his heels. He then proceeds to break off every bar faster than I can stand up again.

"Thank you. Thank you, Duna," I whisper under my breath.

I jump as Titus arrives at my side and begins pulling off our bars while the guard watches helplessly, his face awash with a dumbstruck impotence that I almost pity. He doesn't even bother unsheathing his sword.

"What's the matter, soldier? Gryphon got your tongue?" taunts the Centaur.

The guard doesn't answer, but gapes at Titus in disbelief. The Centaur yanks the key from his neck.

"Now a Centaur's got your key, you old poltroon," he says, waving it in the air before sliding it around his own neck.

"General...your eyes," the guard says, pointing at Titus's face as the general flings the final bar to the ground.

I look up to see the general's copper eyes shining brightly as thought they'd never been beaten at all. In fact, he looks as though he's just awoken from a rejuvenating nap.

"Phulax, perhaps you are not as strong as you think," replies Titus.

I catch myself unwittingly imitating the sentry's bewildered expression.

"Come on then," says Titus, stepping into the corridor separating our cell from the Centaur's. "You too, Centaur," he adds gruffly, then strides out of the prison.

The Centaur furrows his brow. "It seems the general has traded his sanity in return for his eyesight," he says to me.

I laugh briefly and then wave at the Centaur to go ahead of me.

"Wait," I say.

I go to the Centaur and lift the key from around his neck and toss it to the confounded sentry who is crouching over the broken bars, examining those still intact, and scratching his head as he mutters incoherently to himself.

"We are leaving Ēlektōr, Phulax. I think you would be wise to do the same. Unless of course you can think of a good story that might persuade Diokles *not* to pummel you to death with those bars."

Phulax's head half nods, half shakes in acknowledgement of my words as he rubs the useless key between his fingers.

"Thank you," he whispers.

Then, without question or objection, the Centaur and I follow Titus out of the caves and into the wake of my answered prayers.

CHAPTER TWENTY-TWO
REVELATION

Though it was well into the morning hours, I never noticed the sun peek over the eastern mountains or lift one ray of light to salute the day; it was as if Duna had his hand on it while whispering to the dawn, "Not yet, not yet...Stay asleep a while longer..."

And although sinister storm clouds followed us and threatened to break loose with erratic rumbles, the only rain we endured was what was needed to fill our water jars and wash the dirt from our faces. I began to assure myself that the thunder was nothing to be afraid of; perhaps it was the voice of Duna, a lion in the heavens, roaring to remind us of his presence while warding off Diokles's men.

I don't know when, but somewhere between the sands of Ēlektōr and the streams of Eirene, Titus set me on the Centaur's back so I could rest.

And in between the starlit mountains, beneath the bashful sun, and atop a beast who has become to me more friend than foe, I had the sweetest sleep – no nightmares, no flashbacks, no disquieting dreams...only ardent emanations of gratitude rising up with every slow, contented breath.

I awaken to the trickling sound of water skipping over rocks and the Centaur's hooves knocking against them. He begins pawing the floor of the stream, stirring up the silt as he cools his legs and underbelly and rids his body of the foaming sweat that covers it.

I swing my right leg over the Centaur's side and slide into the water, and then plop down into it, splashing the general next to me.

"I didn't dream it," I say, looking up at him. "Your eyes really were healed. It was Carya, you know. She sang in our cell before you woke up."

Titus kneels down and cups a drink of water in his hands.

"It felt like hot fingertips were touching my eyelids. But when I opened them, all I saw were the bars on the ground in front of you. It was all a miracle, wasn't it?" he says. Clearly he isn't fully convinced that our escape wasn't a dream, or perhaps a hallucination induced by the incense filling the cella.

"I can think of no other explanation," I answer. Titus pats me on the shoulder.

"It's good to be out of there. Now just promise me you won't do that again," he says.

"Do what again?"

"Yeah. Do what again?" interrupts the Centaur as he snags a floating branch and begins to chew on its yellowish green leaves.

"You know very well you weren't yourself inside the temple. I could see it in your eyes...you were under his spell," Titus says.

"I – I don't know," I confess. "I felt like I was in the presence of a god, of someone – or something – that could tell me anything I wanted to know, and anything *anyone* wanted to know, for that matter. I was in a state of complete peace." I stand from the water and begin walking toward the bank.

"I'd be willing to wager that aunt of yours once felt the same way," Titus mutters to himself, but I hear him just the same. I pray silently that Diokles was lying about Corinna, that the Gryphon has always been a Gryphon, not a wayfaring woman who let herself be welded into a weapon, a wanton pawn...

How similar we are, my aunt and I. Orphans, both of us. Ashers alike. Carrying an untamed burden that could prove either a blessing or a curse. Drawn to Ēlektōr, to rebellion and anarchy, like wild bees are drawn to rhododendrons, unaware that the nectar they drink is lethal. The only difference between us is she had no one to warn her. No loved ones' prayers to follow her. She drank the poison, and, it would appear to me, for the price of her soul.

"Then how did you end up in prison if you think Diokles to be Apollo incarnate?" the Centaur asks, following me into the spotty shade of a strawberry tree.

"What do know about Apollo?" Titus asks the Centaur.

"The Pythonians worship him as their coming king – the long-awaited *savior of the world*," the Centaur says in a sonorous, singsong voice as he lifts his arms and wiggles his fingers at his sides.

"You say it as if you don't believe it," remarks Titus.

"Of course I don't believe it!" snaps the Centaur as he rears up onto his hind legs and combs the tree for berries. "The gods! The gods!" he says, dancing around like a comedic actor hungry for applause. Then he stops, his visage taking on a look of humorless intensity.

"If you hear nothing else from a Centaurian brute, hear this," he begins. "The gods do not exist. I have served Python all my life. Have I ever seen him, ever heard his voice? Not once. And no one has. He is made up. Just like your great Duna. All the gods compose a made-up mythos meant to make us think there is something out there. That life has meaning."

"I wouldn't be so quick to mock what you do not understand," advises Titus. "If it wasn't for Duna empowering Iris, you would still be in that cell counting the hundreds of fleas jumping off your mangy hide like rats off a sinking ship."

The Centaur can't help but laugh at the general's joke. "I still haven't figured out that trick..." he says to me, itching the serpent tattoo on the back of his sun-burned head.

Titus rolls his eyes and hands me a half dozen berries from a low-hanging branch.

"In answer to your question, Centaur," I say in between bites of the sweet, succulent fruit, "I ended up in prison because I fled the temple after Diokles announced my death sentence."

The Centaur begins to caw wildly and flap his arms like wings. "The belly of the Gryphon too much to *stomach*, eh?" he jests. "The guards at the prison were looking forward to it!"

"Why didn't you lie, general?" I say, ignoring the Centaur's imbecilic behavior, fresh nutrients and sleep now stimulating my thoughts. "Why did you tell Diokles the truth, that I was with Tycho after he killed Patroclus, and that he was able to escape? You knew the truth would mean my execution..." I throw the rest of my berries on the ground, my appetite disappearing as my suspicion grows.

"Did you want me to die, Titus? Perhaps you would have gained special favor with the gods and a great reward from Diokles for offering me, 'the girl who can make gem-bearing goddesses appear' for sacrifice to Python... or Apollo...whomever!" I shout.

"Have you so easily forgotten what Tycho told you?" Titus says calmly.

Trust me... His comforting voice whispers in my mind. I shake my head at Titus.

"I remember," I reply.

"I didn't tell you *all* that Carya told me that night she appeared to me in the cella and gave me that emerald," Titus says as the Centaur gathers my rejected berries and pops them into his mouth.

"Go on," I say. "There are no secrets now, general. We've come too far."

Titus nods and closes his eyes, concentrating to remember the rest of the messenger's words.

"'All Petrodians are drawn to darkness; their pride shuts out the light,
Iris must see the truth for herself, then make a choice to fight.
If to prison you are taken, do not become downcast,
For Duna shall be there in your midst; and no affliction long can last.'"

Titus looks at me with a mixture of remorse and unrepentant resolve as he waits for my response. I turn from him and sit down against the tree. Staring off at the Centaur who smiles at a butterfly poised delicately on his forefinger, I marvel at the picture – the startling profundity – of pure, innocent beauty visiting the ugly, iniquitous, and outcast.

"What faith you have in the riddles of a nymph," I say softly.

"No, Soukina. What faith I have in Duna," he answers. "I didn't know the future. I didn't know for certain that we would be delivered alive from that prison, but I made a decision to believe what Carya said."

"And why didn't you tell me all of this before, when we were coming down the path from the fortress?"

"Would you have followed me to the temple had you known my plan was simply to let Diokles cast his judgment and feed you to the Gryphon?" Titus replies.

You know you wouldn't have, my mind tells me.

"I suppose I would have fled," I say.

"Yes, and gotten yourself captured and killed within minutes."

"I didn't have the faith you did," I admit. "I suppose that's why I was so easily entranced by Diokles. And why Corinna was..."

"What I have learned, Soukina, is that each revelation we obtain in life, no matter how small, brings a burden along with it – the burden of a personal response.

We can take the revelation and act upon it, gain wisdom from it, or we can walk away from it and trust that we are our own best counselors, our own gods."

"I believe I've had a revelation, general. And I know my response."

Titus smiles. "I would very much like to hear it."

I take a breath, and breathing out declare, "Killing innocent people should never be a means to an end. Even if Diokles dies, I will never return to Ēlektōr."

⸻ ◊/◊/◊ ⸻

While Titus and the Centaur slept, I prayed with my eyes wide open and admired the sunlight shimmering like diamonds dancing along the stream, basked in the bath of its rays splashed on my neck and face, and listened to the jangling song of a nearby bunting interspersed with a warbler's harmonizing bursts.

I'd felt the sun, seen its light, and heard birds sing almost every day of my life, but today seemed like the first time I'd experienced any of it. Somehow the light shone a little brighter the moment I started to pray. The sun's warmth felt more like the presence of a most loving entity. The birds' duet sounded like a paean unto heaven. And somehow I felt that I too played a part, if only by virtue of my presence.

Duna, only you can bring justice to my brother. All else has failed me. I place myself as an instrument – no, a weapon – in your hands.

The hours seemed like minutes; if not for my mission still left undone, I would have been content to stay in that place forever. But as the birds stopped their singing and retired to their nests, the Centaur and general awoke, and together we strode toward the Eirenian gates, toward the festival where I will see Acheron again, and where he will be burned alive as Jasper was. And my hands will be the torch.

CHAPTER TWENTY-THREE
THERISMOS

Once inside the city, we are greeted first by the agora. This tremendous marketplace is as busy and vivacious as it was when I left it three years ago, the night I followed my arrested brother and his captors seventy miles south to Enochos. Merchants and craftsmen stand before their booths selling a cornucopia of goods, ranging from odorous leeks and garlic to perfumes, honey jars, and figurines. Other artists and potters work diligently at their stations beneath the stoa, a marble and limestone porch lined with august Ionic columns, the spiral, scroll-like capitals of which suggest its appeal to creative hands and studious minds alike.

The only thing that is different from the way it was three years ago is the disapproving looks the general and I receive from our fellow Eusebians, repulsed by the sight – and smell, no doubt – of the Centaur. We pretend not to notice, and I laugh to myself as the Centaur nods his head and winks at each of the women that pass by.

"It's a good thing I cleaned myself up in the river, isn't it?" he says to the general and me as he strokes his stubbly chin.

"That reminds me," Titus says, hastily pulling a short rope from his belt. He loops it around the Centaur's neck, ties a tight knot, and begins to lead him through the street. "It looks suspicious to have you roaming free, accompanying a pair of respectable Eusebians," he jokes. "Just play along, will you?"

The Centaur snorts and rolls his eyes. "With all due *respect,* general, you will owe me as many sausages and honey cakes as I like for the rest of my days."

I soon begin to notice that up and down the wide street, behind and between every booth, young boys and girls run with sunshine bouncing off the apples of their smiling cheeks as they merrily wave myrtle and willow twigs.

"What's going on?" the Centaur asks.

"You have been away a while, haven't you," Titus says. "Everyone is preparing for Therismos."

"The Feast of the Harvest," I add.

For every Eusebian, children most of all, it is the happiest time of the year. Though I haven't celebrated the Feast in years, just seeing the children gamboling about spontaneously sends a child-like thrill and a bittersweet ache through my body...

Jasper and I couldn't wait for the arrival of autumn when our father would wake us up before dawn and lead us into the sleepy evergreen forest where we'd forage tree branches, sticks, and leaves until lunch time. All afternoon we remained outside, using the materials we'd gathered to build a booth for us all to dwell in throughout Therismos. Meanwhile, our mother enjoyed the solitude of her hearth as she cooked a seasonal soup of squash, cabbage, and garden peas and baked a dessert of sesame and poppy seeds, hazelnuts and honey which formed a texture and taste so divine that my mouth still waters at the thought of it.

The first morning of the seven-day feast, our father would summon my brother and me outside the new shelter and recite the poem he'd written when Jasper was born to illustrate the reason why we celebrated and slept in the primitive shelter; we couldn't run amok inside of it until we listened...

"It happened thousands of years ago, in a far-away winter land,
Our ancestors fled a tyrant's rule, guided by light from Duna's hand.
They marched toward this fair and fertile coast, freed forever from whip and chain,
But they feared the giants that dwelled here – how fast their faith in him did wane.
Duna was angered by their mumblings, and made them wander forty years,
'Til the doubting generation died, and took away with them their fears.
But all the while, he provided, sent them fire and bread each day,
And they slept sound inside their shelters, until called to set out on their way...
When they saw the walls of the giants, not a one did cower or quake,
For a Man of Duna came to them and said the city was theirs to take.
In obedience they trumpeted, never raising a sword or shield;
At sound of blast and sight of faith did the entire city yield.
The walls shook and crumbled to the sea; our weary feet would no more roam,
As we now celebrate our harvest, we remember our former home...
Within those huts, underneath the stars, we felt forgiveness, tasted grace,
And that is a story of stories that no one shall ever erase."

It is when my attention is caught by the cheerful *witt-witt!* of a swallow perched atop the cornice crowning the stoa that my longing for childhood is dismissed. I suddenly ask the question:

"Do you think Tycho is inside the stoa, general? Perhaps we should go search for him. He'd like to know we're all right."

"Tycho...I know that name," says the Centaur.

"I'm sure you do. He is – *was* – a Pythonian like you," I reply.

The Centaur's eyes stare ahead blankly as his ruddy complexion grows pale.

"Oh no. He was a Petrodian of a different sort. I was nothing more than a bad-tempered child compared to the likes of Tycho. He was one of the few men whose evil made me think perhaps Python really does exist."

"What do you mean? What has he done?" I ask.

"I don't think the general would find it appropriate for me to divulge the details to an innocent young woman like you," answers the Centaur.

"I'm not innocent!" I argue. "I am responsible for the deaths of four Eusebians whose only crime was not bowing to Diokles. Their blood is on my hands, Centaur. I am no better than Tycho."

"Nor am I," interjects Titus, turning to us with watery eyes. "Had I not been such a coward, I never would have sent the psiloi after Ireneus, and I certainly wouldn't have assigned you to the Gryphon."

My heart tightens, and I clench the general's arm.

"It's all right, general. What is important now is that we aren't cowards anymore. I'm sorry I brought up the past. It doesn't do any of us any good," I say.

The general nods his head and clears his throat, reassuming a soldierly stance.

"Thank you, Iris. And the Centaur is right. It will not benefit us to hear of Tycho's past either. No matter what egregious crimes or heinous acts is he guilty of, he has been forgiven by Duna. He serves him now."

"You make the man sound like a faultless priest!" the Centaur remarks.

"That's it!" As the words exit out of my mouth, my legs carry me like wings to the ancient heart of my homeland beating within it: the Eusebian Temple.

◈◈◈

I feel like Icarus as the wings I'd imagined carrying me across the agora melt like wax when I come to what is known by Eusebians simply as the "bathing place." *How could I forget...*

The bathing place is a rectangular rock-cut pool fed by the waters of the Maqor Spring which flows into it from the city's two main aqueducts. Before anyone can enter the precincts of the Temple, they must be immersed in the pool as a ritual act of purification.

On the final day of Therismos, my family and I would come here along with all of Eirene and patiently wait our turn to step into the pool. As we waited, our father reminded us to ponder the past twelve months and silently list the things that had made us spiritually unclean. "You will go into it a peasant, and rise out of it a queen," he encouraged me. Meanwhile, the Alpha guards looked down on us all with derisive eyes and supercilious smiles, their full armor and puffed-up chests reminding us, the vanquished "peasants", to remember our place.

Back then it was difficult for me to name the wrongs I'd done; I was well-behaved most of the time, obeyed our teachers and studied my lessons, and hardly ever told a lie. Even as slave to my brother's murderer, I did my duty without disdain. But my actions since the night at Okeanos, when I gripped a Soukinoi blade, belie my innocence. I realize now that the darkness I've brought to this world was within me all along. I could only repress it for so long after my life fell into ruins.

Today, as I stare into the crystal waters and the hunter's eyes reflecting back at me, my mind is flooded with the turbid profusion of my trespasses. From defying Duna to his face in The Great Sea to delivering a tortuous death to guiltless Ireneus, I fear there is not enough water in all of Petros to make me pure again.

"Stop tarrying, Iris!" The voice like Alexa's that I heard on the mountain top with the Gryphon shouts inside my head. "Forget about Tycho. Do what you came here to do!"

"Acheron," I whisper, slowly stepping foot onto the pool's first step.

"Can you hurry up, please?" I hear a child's voice ask from behind me. I turn to see a red-headed girl holding her mother's hand.

"I'm sorry. She's a bit eager to get to the festival," says her mother.

"The festival!" the voice returns. "The Guardians are at the Temple during the festival – *Acheron* is at the Temple!"

My heart rate quickens. My hands sweat. My mouth goes try. I take a deep breath and lower my other foot onto the step.

"She's very polite. My apologies for making you wait. I haven't been here in a while," I say, noticing that an endless line has formed behind them. "Here I go!" I smile at the girl, then dive headlong into the pool with a splash, no longer fretting about the state of my soul.

CHAPTER TWENTY-FOUR
INDIGO

I scurry around the periphery of the Eusebian Court, jumping carefully from one shadow to the next, trying my best to ignore the white-robed figures of the priests whose imperturbable demeanors and humbly bowed heads sicken my stomach with thoughts of Ireneus. Each one carries armfuls of large red branches and sickle-shaped willow leaves to be placed around the holy altar where it is said Duna first breathed life into man. It is also the place on which a band of vandalizing Alphas once scattered the carved-off hooves and chopped-off tails of dead Centaurs as blasphemous sacrifices to our "silly, jealous god."

It was for beseeching Acheron over the unclean offerings that my brother and the others were murdered. Rather than putting an end to the desecration, my master ordered one-hundred thousand drachmae from the Temple treasury instead, an amount it would take a Eusebian nearly four lifetimes of labor to earn. The city retaliated not with force, but with mockery, matching the offenders' crime; they sent a beggar's basket around the agora to fill with coins for our presumably impoverished Guardian. Little did they know what the price would be for such impudence: the bodies of five of their sons, burned alive on Enochos, a sea filled more with ashes and tears than water.

"Iris!" a voice calls out from the immaculate columned aisles. But when I turn, I see no one.

I continue walking through at a brisker pace, gripping my dagger as though Acheron could present himself at any moment.

*You're very close now, Iris. Be ready...*the voice inside me warns.

"My lady!" It isn't Acheron at all.

Tycho.

I begin to run towards the sound.

"Tycho? Where are you?" Now I am in the sunshine, standing in the midst of the unroofed court, hoping my mind is not playing tricks on me.

My eyes skim the clusters of families around me. It appears every man has either an arm wrapped around his wife's waist or a child atop his shoulders.

Where is he?

I feel a hand rest itself on my shoulder. I look at it and see that it is nearly completely covered by a long white, priestly sleeve.

"My lady," whispers the voice.

I turn to see Tycho, his broad smile gleaming in the noonday sun.

"You answer to it now," he says.

"It's what you insist on calling me. I suppose I'll get used to it one day," I smile back, surprised by just how happy I feel to see him.

"You're – you're a priest?" I ask him, as he takes my hand in each of his and squeezes it so tight that I think my fingers will break.

"It's my disguise," he says. "A rather good one, don't you think?"

I laugh. "Yes. I thought I was being haunted there in the colonnade."

"I'm sorry. I didn't want to follow you inside and make anyone suspicious. Congregating with Soukinoi is not a priestly duty, you know," he winks.

"I'm not a Soukina anymore, Tycho. I can't bear to think about what might have happened had I stayed there a day longer."

Tycho's smile fades from his lips and rises into his eyes where it lightly traces the topaz inside them, like sunlight framing the clouds.

"Thank Duna," he sighs, his enlivened eyes looking heavenward. "Come with me," he says, lessening his grip on my hand as he pulls me after him.

"Wait. What about Titus?" I ask, looking frantically around the court for his tanned face towering above the others, or for the Centaur's tail swatting irritably at the air. "And the Centaur..." I whisper, remembering that Centaurs are prohibited from the Temple's inner courts.

"Meet me at the woodshed just over there in three minutes. Trust me," Tycho says. And I don't ask another question.

━━━━◦◦◦◦━━━━

The woodshed, situated at the northeastern quadrant of the Eusebian Court, was completely empty. The priests consigned to menial tasks had finished sorting the good willow wood from the detestable, and all that was left were forsaken piles of discarded, worm-eaten branches judged unfit for the altar.

I waited for Tycho only a few moments. As he approached I listened to him quietly singing along with the priests assembled somewhere I could not see, somewhere above me like wood nymphs hidden in the trees. The timbre of the priests' voices harmonizing with harps, lyres, cymbals, and flutes was unlike anything I'd ever heard before, as if their music had been traveling tirelessly through the dissonant eons of time, destined to arrive here in this Temple at this very moment...

"How great are your works; we remember all that you have done,
You set us free from bondage and gave us hope of a Promised One.
Those who sow tears today shall reap joy and song tomorrow,
We trust you, Duna, our eternal King, to rid us again of sorrow.
Unless you build our walls, we labor here in vain;
Hear our prayers, heal our land, and restore us once again."

This song was one of many sung every year on the final day of Therismos to express thanksgiving to Duna for freeing our people once before and for faithfully providing an abundant autumn harvest ever since. But I couldn't help but notice how Tycho changed the words, albeit ever so slightly:

"You set us free from bondage and sent us your Promised One."

Most Eusebians consider Phos just another charlatan, another failed pseudo-*christos*, or "anointed one." But not Tycho.

I didn't have to ask him why; I knew the reason is that he, like Jasper, believes Phos was the one of whom the Oracles spoke and the priests sing. Phos' death in the Great Sea was the greatest paradox in of all Petrodian history. His defeat was, to Jasper and the other disciples, an everlasting and irrefutable victory...over iniquity, over sickness, over evil, over death.

And yet here I am, a guilt-stained Eusebian woman infected with an all-consuming lust for vengeance because of the cold-blooded Alpha Guardian who took my brother's life.

Where is victory?

When I step into the Indigo Chamber behind Tycho, I spot one man who appears to have been waiting for me, ready to answer such questions as that. But unlike Diokles, the skin of this learned man neither dances with the energy of mystic vapors, nor sparkles with the capricious anointing of Apollo. His face is deeply wrinkled and ashen, like thin papyrus starting to decay, and his gait is stiff and slow, yet not without dignity as he holds his shoulders back and deftly adjusts his turban, at the front of which is fastened a flower-shaped plate of pure gold.

"My dear," he says to me, with the rich, orotund voice of a much younger man. "Welcome to Eirene. Tycho tells me it's been three years since you've been home."

Home. All this time I thought I didn't have one; all the people of my home are dead. And who knows what's become of our house and the tannery; both have probably been burned to the ground to purge the air of its putrid smells. But then again, this city is my home. It is as much a part of me as my family, and the earth on which it is built cannot be destroyed – not by any man, at least.

"It is good to be home," I smile softly.

"Iris, this is Anatolius," says Tycho. "He has graciously given me sanctuary here."

"And for you," adds the priest.

Anatolius turns and leads us to the front of the room, above which a giant silk cloth of indigo hangs and traverses the width of the chamber, rolling like a wave as a passive breeze sails across it.

This indigo "veil" as it is called, is said to represent the perennial barrier between Petros and heaven, between man and his creator. Each year on the Day of Katallagé, or, "reconciliation," the high priests take down the veil, sprinkle the blood of the purest lambs and bulls upon it, then carry it into the Eusebian Court where they hold it by its corners, and, along with all of Eirene, plead with Duna to forgive them for another year of falling short of his holiness.

> *"We hide not our transgressions; we lay each one at your feet,*
> *To mingle with the blood of lambs and with your justice meet.*
> *Look favorably on our contrite hearts, forgive us, and make us new,*
> *So that when fire falls and flood waters rise, we can run once more to you."*

"I'm sure Diokles has already sent his assassins for both of us," Tycho says to me. "I haven't stopped praying for you and the general since I last saw you at Ēlektōr."

The general...Where is Titus?

"I have asked one of the attendants to bring food for you, Iris. I assume you are hungry?" Anatolius asks.

My stomach growls in response. Somehow the task of escaping the desert and reuniting with Tycho had distracted me from hunger, but now, all I can focus on is my body's need for rest and a solid meal. But first...

"Where are the others? General Titus and the Centaur?" I ask.

The high priest and Tycho look at one another, trying to determine which of them should answer.

"The Centaur isn't permitted on the Temple grounds, I'm afraid," Anatolius says. "Not yet, at least. With Duna's help, things will be changing here, but it will take some time."

The attendant enters from the eastern door carrying a plate of bread and meat and melon. Anatolius motions for me to sit in the chair at the center of the Chamber, the only chair in the room.

"That is your seat, sir," I say, lowering myself onto the stone ground.

"Nonsense. Tycho help her up," Anatolius insists, his eyes twinkling as though he is partaking in some sort of outlawed mischief. But I suppose he is. "I told you things will be changing. Making it permissible for a hungry orphaned woman to be served supper in Duna's house while sitting in a proper chair is at the top of the list," he smiles as Tycho pulls me to my feet, the serpent tattoo peeking out of his sleeve.

I pause for a few seconds more, then proceed to sit in the chair where the attendant is waiting for me. He hands me the platter and then exits the way he came, into the light and music.

My mouth waters just holding the warm plate from which the smell of wheat arises, an expensive grain that even Acheron only demanded when he was especially inebriated. I want so much to lower my head until it is within mere inches of it and, without reserve, shamelessly break it apart and devour it one fistful at a time. But instead, I struggle to slow down my jaws, savor each bite as best I can, and wait patiently for someone to speak candidly about the status of the others.

"Between the Guardians and Diokles's men, the Centaur has only enemies here," says Tycho. "The general did not want to abandon him in the agora. They've gone somewhere where it is safe for him."

"Diokles ordered that the Centaur be left unharmed," I say, remembering how curious it was – and is – to me that Diokles would let him live, and live painlessly at that.

"Ah, of course," sighs Anatolius. "Because of Apollo. He and the other cultists respect the Centaurs– begrudgingly so – because they believe Apollo fathered the very first, Centaurus. But nevertheless, the Guardians will not be so tolerant. Having Petrodian Centaurs running loose during Therismos doesn't make things easy for them. Better for the city to be as calm as possible so that they can keep a closer eye on us, hmm?"

"Wait," I say, nodding thanks to the attendant who returns with a cup of water for me. "Go back to Apollo. Is it true what he thinks? Did the Centaur race descend from Apollo?"

"Apollo...Python...yes. Those are different names for the same person, the Evil One who rebelled against Duna in the primordial ages before us. The one whose expulsion from Duna's presence created the indigo void between Petros and heaven, chaos and cosmos," explains the high priest, his eyes scanning the indigo veil as though they are watching Duna's hands now laying it heavily between our realms, spreading it out tautly from east to west, separating this cursed rock, this *petros*, from his glory.

"The dark ones who fell with him created hybrid beings, beasts like the Harpies and sphinxes. Creatures remarkably strong and full of hatred that would be able to defeat Duna's son. Python has known his destiny all along, and all along he has been plotting to change it, using the hybrids to terrorize and intimidate, Alphas to tyrannize and dispirit, and even our own people to deceive and confuse."

"Even I was swept into his strategy," Tycho says. "First by taking the tattoo of Python, and then the scar of the Soukinoi." We each turn over our right hands and examine the dagger's line drawn across it.

"When you told me at Ourania that you had been serving someone who claimed to have all the power in the world, you were speaking of Diokles, weren't you?" I ask.

Tycho nods. "Yes. The *power* is from Python. As Anatolius has said, the Evil One is energizing both the Pythonians and the Soukinoi, though neither one realizes it, as *I* never realized it."

"And what about my power?" I ask. "I suppose Python wanted that, too."

"You're speaking of the doma you possess," answers Anatolius. "The Ashers' gifts are extremely valuable to Python, and by extension, to Diokles. If the doma is not protected, not entrusted to Duna to nurture and direct, the Asher becomes easy prey for evil to take hold of."

"It took hold of my aunt, Corinna," I say. "She had the gift of flight, and today she is the Gryphon. I've watched her tear apart holy men like yourself without hesitation. Her thirst for blood is never satisfied." My eyes fill with tears and I set down my plate.

"I am sorry, Iris," says Anatolius, his voice tender with sympathy. "Python's forces have always promised Ashers the world in return for their gifts. And for a time, many of them experience wealth and pleasure beyond their wildest dreams. Some, much like your aunt it sounds to me, suffer immediately; their corruptor doesn't bother masquerading as a beneficent emissary or selfless tutor. Either way, the outcome is the same: Python's plans are carried out, and the Asher..."

He doesn't need to finish his explanation. I know what happens to the Asher who surrenders his doma to Python. I've seen it for myself, inside the hollow, vitreous eyes of my aunt who has not an inkling that I am her sister's daughter, and, if Diokles succeeds, her next victim.

"It's good you are here, Iris," Anatolius continues. "It's been our prayer, since Tycho arrived, that your power might be placed in Duna's hands, while there is still time."

"Time? Time until what?" I ask, my hands so cold and my heart so heavy that I wonder if the doma is still with me.

My mind flashes back to the morning I discovered Niobe lying dead on Acheron's floor. I couldn't use the doma to devastate his home and deliver a warning; the harder I tried, the weaker I felt. Could it be that Duna was restraining it, protecting me from moving one step closer to a fate like Corinna's? But hadn't my fate been to join the Soukinoi and avenge my brother? Now I'm not so sure...

"Time until the Soukinoi or Pythonians, or maybe both, converge here," Anatolius says, his gaze drifting out the door. "At any hour. That is what the Oracles foresaw."

"Diokles told me they were planning an attack here," I say, my words sounding weak, garbled, and far away, as if I'm speaking from the bottom of the bathing place or the farthest reaches of an Elektor cave. "To destroy the Guardians."

"No, Iris," Tycho says, coming near to me. "They want to destroy *us*. Acheron, the Python worshipers, the Soukinoi... They all want to obliterate Eirene to make way for their peace-bringing ruler. They want to stamp out any trace of Phos and his disciples, starting here. Starting with us."

CHAPTER TWENTY-FIVE
TESTIMONY

Outside in the Eusebian Court, everybody dances and twirls to the sound of pipes, drums, and tambourines. The children wave purple banners over their heads and hop up and down and side to side when they can't keep the rhythm. Daring entertainers do back flips, juggle fruit then flaming torches, stealing the breath of both young and old - but all I see in the spectacle is a shadow of Enochos...the five burning pyres and the smoke of their slaughter.

Tycho and I sit together just outside the Chamber door and stare in silence at the florescent euphoria pulsing around us like a sky designed by children's dreams. The colors, the music, the dancing and jubilation... the longer I watch, the more heartsick I feel. They are all ignorant of the darkness buried far below the surface of the Alphas' hubris, their disgust with Eusebian piety, the darkness that transcends even the indigo chasm cut between Duna and Petros, and the rivers of catastrophes still flowing from it. I have only heard the faintest whispers of the Evil One's plan, and this limited knowledge alone makes me shudder.

Perhaps it is best that they don't know, I think. Yes. If I were here with my parents and with Jasper, all of us healthy and unharmed, I would prefer not to know of doom and destruction and malevolent plans. And even if I was told or heard rumors in the air, I would probably keep on dancing.

My gaze shifts to Anatolius making his way across the court toward the nearby Maqor Spring, carrying a golden flask at his chest. When he returns, there will be a libation of water and a prayer for rain as the people recite the words:

"We draw water from your wells of mercy, sip life from your springs of salvation.
We give thanks for the rainfall in dry, desert places, the harvest amid desolation ..."

"How do you know Anatolius?" I ask Tycho, my mind trying to distract itself from the ominous verse of the Oracles.

"I was told to come here and find him, before I met you at Okeanos with Lysander." Tycho begins, his eyes watching the priest's white robes disappear down the steps of the western gate.

"Who told you to find him? Carya? I know she told you to go with Lysander that night, even though you had already recanted your vows to Diokles in your heart."

Tycho runs his hand through his hair, something he does when he's nervous or unsure.

"Tell me, Tycho. Why can't you trust me? I followed you here, didn't I?"

I loosen the pouch on my girdle and pull out the emerald stone.

"Look," I say, spreading my palm for him to see the resplendent gem. "Carya instructed the general to give this to me *only* if I forgave him for executing my brother. She said it symbolizes a new beginning for me. I want to find the new beginning, Tycho."

Tycho lowers his hand from his head and places it on mine. The warmth of our fingers interlocking surges up my arm and into my cheeks; I turn my face away from him.

"The prayers of your family go before you, Iris. They've led you all this way because Duna heard them and he honored them – he honors them still."

I turn my face back toward his and smile as a gentle wind blows against us.

"And I do trust you," Tycho continues. "But the answer to your question...I'm not sure you will believe it."

I frown and slip my hand away from his. I've seen so much; how can he think that I am a skeptic now?

"Phos appeared to me, Iris. Days before I met you, I was traveling to Enochos intent on killing the 'weak ones,' as Diokles called them – any Eusebians who were followers of the Hodos, who believed that Phos was Duna's anointed son. I was being used by the Evil One, yet again, to destroy my own people, one mission at a time. That is how much he hates us."

My mind swarms with questions, but the first flies out of my mouth like an angry wasp:

"Acheron killed followers of the Hodos. He murdered my brother. Diokles kills them, too?! *You* killed them, too?!"

You can't trust anyone, Iris. Not even Tycho, the voice inside me hisses, the voice that speaks for the unrelenting side of myself still dominated by wrath.

I start to stand, but Tycho gently grasps my arm.

"Please, Iris. It is true, and I am sorry, but you must understand that Diokles does this because he is deceived, as I was deceived. He schemes and kills and terrorizes because he is a servant of the Evil One; he believes Apollo will soon reveal himself and reward him for his faithfulness in the coming age. The Hodos stand in the way."

"How can a few religious Eusebians stop an immortal god from claiming dominion?" I scoff, watching Anatolius's attendant pick up a fair-haired toddler and spin her around, again and again, a dandelion floating buoyantly in the stream of a summer breeze.

"It isn't our beliefs that can stop him. It's our oneness with Duna because of Phos. Because we have accepted that his sacrifice has cleansed us, we carry the power that raised him within us. And *that* is what the Evil One fears. He trembles every time we assert that power, every time we speak with the authority of Phos. I could feel the darkness inside me shrinking in panic when I heard his voice that night..."

"When you heard Phos, who *died* seven years ago?" I ask, unable to bridle my mordant mood.

Tycho takes a deep sigh.

"I thought Phos was dead, too. But he isn't, Iris. That is something we must all believe by faith."

"Faith? He appeared to you! If he's so powerful, why doesn't he appear in the agora or here at the Temple and show us he's alive himself?!"

My emotions will not allow me to sit here a second longer. I get up and storm into the Chamber, glad to find it empty and silent, save for the whispering indigo veil undulating in the vault above me. I stand beneath it, close my eyes, and calm my breathing.

Acheron. Find Acheron!

The voice is growing louder.

You didn't escape from your master and come all this way to be softened by some sanctimonious proselyte! You are stronger than this!

I look up into the veil, now a sheet of midnight sky in the dreary absence of sunlight. Just this morning, I felt as though I was one of the exultant birds singing around me, a bunting perched on her limb, eagerly coaxing the dawn out of its slumber, a dawn promised to bring the culmination of my mission. But now, in the surreal stillness of this Chamber, I feel like a much lowlier animal, an ant perhaps. A resourceful, obdurate creature that collects, carries, and constructs, spellbound by its own skill, enamored by its brawn, impelled by its own shortsighted ambition.

The ant is *"its own best counselor, its own god"...* The words of Titus silence the vociferous demands of the inner voice.

"I'm not a Soukina," I say aloud, just as I said it to Titus earlier today.

"Then what are you?" I can hear him reply, the thought of it almost audible.

"Iris."

It's Tycho, but I keep my back to him and stare at the Chamber's west-facing door, resisting the voice in my head commanding me to barge through it and do what I came here to do.

"Iris, please listen to me. You asked why Phos doesn't appear to us all, and the fact is I don't know," Tycho says. "What I *do* know is that Duna chose to place him in my path, the path of a man who scourged and murdered innocent men, imprisoned their wives and children, and sold many of them as slaves to the Guardians simply because of their faith.

"For three days I saw nothing but darkness because the light in which he appeared to me was too brilliant for human eyes. It struck me with death and life all at once. I felt what it is like to be separated from Duna for eternity, and it is something I would never in a million years wish on my worst enemy. It was unbearable, unescapable. I saw the blackness of the world with neither physical nor spiritual sight. That a man such as I could be touched and changed seems sufficient proof that Phos is he who claimed to be, does it not?"

"Anatolius trusts you. I find that in itself to be miraculous," I admit.

"Yes. Reluctantly," Tycho laughs a little. "Phos told him I would come here. It was he who laid his hands on me the night I regained my vision. I was reborn that night."

I vividly remember the night Jasper came home, *"reborn."* He hadn't been intercepted on the road by Phos as Tycho was, or healed by one of Duna's messengers like I was. He had merely been eating lunch on a hillside not far from the Temple when a man began to testify to the circles of families and friends gathered on the grass.

This man had once been called the Striks, named so after the savage owl of Alpha myth that disemboweled its victims and relished the blood of infants. The ghost story circulated that this Striks had incarnated itself into a deranged Eusebian man who noiselessly stalked the streets of Eirene, picking up the scent of the most unsuspecting souls, mewing at their doors like a neglected cat, and then cutting them down with sharp, sadistic claws before they could glimpse his face. Just before dusk, he'd return to the tombs outside the city where he would cut himself with stones, sniveling and shrieking through the daylight hours until he could hunt again.

The Striks said that one day he saw Phos a great distance away, and the evil inside of him thrust him out of the tombs, took control of his limbs, and sent him running full speed in his direction.

"What are you doing here, Phos, son of almighty Duna? I beg you, do not torment me!" the Striks whimpered.

"What is your name?" Phos asked not the Striks, but the force that possessed him.

"My name is Phalanx," boasted the Striks. "For we are many. We are an army that has claimed this body!"

"But the army of evil within me was no match for the power Phos carried," reported the man, no longer a monster, but an honest blacksmith, a husband and father.

"Had it not been for the scars that covered his body," Jasper said, "no one would have believed that he was the same man. Phos won the victory over Python in that man's life, Iris. I believe he has won such victory for all of us."

And so Jasper's life was changed forever because he had faith to take this man at his word, to believe that he truly had been delivered by Duna's son. And as I stand here, listening to the story of yet another transformed Pythonian, I know that I must make a choice, not just to believe, but to *accept.*

But before I can utter a word to Tycho, a trumpet blasts from the Temple pinnacle overlooking the city. Ten quick, reverberating bursts: a call to arms, a call to retreat.

CHAPTER TWENTY-SIX
INVASION

G o...that way!" Tycho shouts, pointing at the western door. I turn and run across the Chamber, push the door open with a grunt, and stand paralyzed by the sight of hundreds of Eusebians fleeing the Temple and flooding the broad street below toward the agora.

"Come on!" Tycho pulls on my arm and heads north along the edge of the colonnade in which he found me. He sheds his white robes as he walks, revealing his plain, brown, threadbare tunic and the conspicuous serpent tattoo.

"Where are we going?" I ask, trying my best to keep up.

"To stop Anatolius from giving the libation. He'll be the first Diokles comes for."

"What about Acheron?"

But Tycho doesn't hear me. Or at least he pretends he doesn't.

My heart jumps as a flock of doves takes flight from the roof above us, their pounding wings momentarily masking a much more terrifying sound...that of siege engines rolling across the bridge through the golden Chrysos Gate.

"The Soukinoi have battering rams?" I ask.

"Politics is a perplexing thing, a machine unto itself," is all Tycho says, leaving my mind to wonder if and how Diokles, who allegedly loathes the Alphas as much as I do, is subsidized by the Guardians, by Acheron...

I see Anatolius in the distance, walking unhurriedly through the gate with the flask of freshly drawn water in his hands. The trumpets blast again. The tree trunks swinging from the siege engines slam into the corners of the Temple walls again, and again, and again, the unremitting rhythm replacing the merry flutes and jovial lyres with a dark, portentous refrain.

Children cry until they are scooped up by their families and carried away to safety – wherever "safety" is – but the high priest continues on with even, purposeful steps toward the Temple altar. His attendant who served me supper runs toward us, white sleeves flapping like the wings of the flustered doves that escaped from the Chamber roof moments ago.

"What is it?" Tycho asks the attendant, though his attention is fixed on Anatolius. He slows his pace to listen to his answer, but only slightly.

"Anatolius pleads with you not to come any further. He sends this message:

'I hold forth the water like the word of life that has been shown to the world and written on our hearts. I rejoice in this day, in knowing that by Duna's grace I have not run this race in vain. Rejoice with me as my life is poured out as an offering to him, just as your continued service shall be a sweet-smelling sacrifice high above the Moonbow.'"

"Anatolius...no..." whispers Tycho, his eyes closing as the rumbling of the battering rams ceases, and the first wall starts to fall. "Tha – thank you," Tycho mumbles to the attendant. "Go now. Find your family and take them to the aqueduct. You'll be safe there."

The attendant hesitates, but one more look of urgency from Tycho sends him on his way. I watch as he disappears under the portico.

"You should go wit – " Tycho begins.

"You know I won't," I say, my eyes darting back and forth from the Chrysos Gate to the trembling eastern tower presently giving way to the engines' loud, unyielding blows.

Acheron is here, Iris. Be patient. Be alert! the voice warns.

As I grip my dagger, I feel the doma's heat returning, flooding my body, then watch as a squadron of at least two hundred war horses trot into the court, their helmeted riders holding either a flaming torch or a steel javelin.

No sound except the jingling of heavy coats of mail and metal-fringed kilts is heard as the cavalry surrounds the inner Court of the Priests on all sides, the Court Anatolius has resolved never to leave.

Tycho and I take off running.

We dash through the portico, duck into a passageway that I assume only a few are privy to, climb up a pitch-black winding staircase, and finally find ourselves on a high rooftop of carved cedar overhanging the Court below. Tycho drops to his knees and elbows and crawls on his belly, grabbing hold of the roof's spiked edge, tipped with gold.

"Anatolius! Come down from there, you fool! The festival has ended, or haven't you noticed!"

I join Tycho and peer over the roof to see the horses funneling one by one into the Court and forming dense, impenetrable rows around the altar. At the center of the altar stands Anatolius, the golden flask held steadfast, sparkling in his hands like a tiny beacon beside a stormy sea; I watch Tycho's eyes yearning to approach the beacon, to save Anatolius, but the sea is unnavigable. There is no way to him.

A man robed in purple dismounts his gray dappled horse and marches up the ramp affixed to the altar. His blond head is crowned with a gilded wreath.

Diokles.

"Anatolius, I do not take pleasure in being ignored!" he shouts.

But Anatolius doesn't turn his head to acknowledge the would-be king. He approaches a silver cup and begins to pour in the libation.

"When the sun sets, we're leaving the way we came, before they burn the Temple," Tycho whispers.

Burn the Temple? That thousands of years of prayer, revelation, worship, and sacrifice could be reduced to dying embers in a single night seems inconceivable. My family has been taken from me, my home is lost, but to my surprise I have felt sincerest comfort in knowing that the place of our traditions and the foundation of our beliefs stands intact. But it seems that even this ancient tabernacle, ordained and designed by Duna himself, is not impervious to Python's plans.

Where is the god who led our people here, displayed his power, crushed the giants, imparted his wisdom, sent his son, placed the Moonbow in the sky, who has promised to bring our people peace?

"Have you gone deaf, old man?!" Diokles jeers.

"Tycho, we have to do something!" I whisper, twisting my hot hands around the spikes.

"There is nothing to be done now. He is in Duna's hands," replies Tycho, placing his hand on mine.

"I can help him with *my* hands…" I say, jerking my hand from beneath Tycho's. Flexing every finger, I watch each wrinkle and crack of my palm fade into the flush of fire welling up from them. But as I steady my arm and squint one eye, bringing my target into better focus, Anatolius begins to speak.

"I shall carry out my duties here as long as there is breath in my lungs. I am a humble servant of Phos. It is upon his rock and with his strength that I stand, and I will not be moved!"

My arm goes numb. My enfeebled fingertips fold in. The Soukinoi shout and curse and shake their javelins. Even when Diokles raises his hand to silence them, they do not stop for several minutes.

"I am not afraid of you who can destroy my flesh!" yells Anatolius as the din dies down. "No, I fear the one who can destroy both soul and body in the abyss."

"It shall be my honor to be the one who sends you there!"

Diokles shoots his right arm up into the air. I hold my breath as two arrows come whizzing down from the opposite tower, straight into the high priest's chest.

Anatolius falls to his knees and lifts his face toward heaven. A hush falls over the Soukinoi as the priest opens his mouth to speak his final words.

"Behold! The heavens are opened and Phos is standing at Duna's right side! I wish you all could see!"

The priest's declaration, robust and full of vigor, repeats itself in piercing echoes throughout the Court. Diokles covers his ears, but I strain to listen as each word penetrates my heart a dozen times, powerful arrows all their own.

As the last syllable fades, Diokles removes his hands from his ears and rushes across the altar, drawing the dagger from his belt. But before he can inflict a final blow, the high priest falls onto his side. Diokles spits, pulls the arrows from the body, and holds them up like trophies for the squadron to celebrate.

As the cavalry cheers, I withdraw from the roof's edge and wilt against the cold stone door. My useless hands curled into fists, I gaze at the indigo veil of starless sky above me and feel, for the first time, as though I am looking into my own heart – a black, empty, lonely hole that shines only with the light of other spheres, which themselves are but shadows of something far greater...

Tycho crawls backwards toward me and smiles at the sky. "I'll see you again, my friend," he says.

"Tycho," I say. "I want to see him again. I want to see what he saw, as he was dying."

Without a second's pause, Tycho whispers loudly, "You can!"

"But how? We have to leave and the Temple is going to be destroyed. I feel like I've become an orphan all over again." I bury my face in my hands.

This is not a time for self-pity, Iris! You are becoming weak!

"No," I say aloud to the inner voice. "I'm not!"

"You're not what?" asks Tycho.

I lift my head, take a deep breath, and before I can talk myself out of it confess:

"I began to hear a voice the day I was assigned to the Gryphon. And another voice, a different voice, the same afternoon. Both nudge me in opposite directions – one towards vengeance and rebellion, the other toward...well...I don't know..."

Tycho raises an eyebrow as he smiles, "Don't you?"

I can't help but smile back. Even as the battering rams resume and streaks of orange flames set fire to the portico, I am in no rush to desert this temporary peak of refuge. What will it benefit me to leave here with my life without settling my soul?

"The other voice nudges me toward Jasper. Toward Anatolius. Toward *you*," I say firmly.

Tycho gives a knowing nod.

"One belongs to your flesh. One belongs to the spirit of Duna. It's his spirit that convicts us of the evil in our hearts and makes us aware of our unworthiness."

"What do I do, Tycho? I cannot sacrifice an animal or purify myself at the bathing place. I – "

"Iris," Tycho stops me as my speech and heart rate quicken together. I take a deep breath and lean my head back against the door.

"You don't need to do *anything*," he says. "Only declare with your mouth that Phos is Duna's son, and believe in your heart that he conquered the grave. Then you will become a new creation, born again. That other voice you hear will have no right to rule you another second. With the spirit of Duna, you and I can conquer anything. All because of his love."

I shake my head and squeeze back tears, my mind struggling to find fairness in this foreign dogma, my own spirit leaping to accept it with faith alone, the same faith that Jasper had...

"It's what the Oracles promised would come and what they longed to see. It's *charis*, Iris...grace...an unmerited gift! Phos died to impute to us *his* righteousness, something we could not earn with an eternity's worth of sacrifices, rituals, and cleansing."

The sun has set but the moon shines just as bright, a holy, radiant spirit filling the desperate, indigo heart.

"I believe," I say, listening as walls both within my heart and around this structure start to crumble. Tycho looks around nervously, but only for a minute; he knows there is nothing more important than hearing these words: "I believe that Phos is the son of Duna. I believe that he rose from the Great Sea. He conquered the grave!"

Tycho has no words. He draws me into his arms and holds me until the destruction comes to an eerie unsettling halt and all we hear are the anguished cries of men and women in torment. We break apart and crawl back to the edge and look down at Diokles watching over three people being flogged by six Soukinoi guards.

Diokles turns around, raises his arms to his sides as if beseeching a god and cries out:

"If the fugitives Iris and Tycho are hiding here, they have two minutes to hand themselves over. That is, of course, if they wish their friends to live!"

CHAPTER TWENTY-SEVEN
TREACHERY

Diokles turns his head and mutters something to the guards. They lower their three-thonged whips, wipe their brows, and step aside from the hostages, each one of them collapsed onto their knees, surrounded by a morbid tessellation of their own crimson blood.

Diokles pulls a rod out of one of the guard's hands and pushes it into the first man's shoulder as he barks a muffled command. Diokles prods him again.

"Gennadius!" shouts the man. "My name is Gennadius!"

I watch as Tycho's tanned face turns white as the moon. I feel my blood, deprived of air and frozen instantaneously by fear, run cold. Because there, in the midst of the altar like an unblemished lamb, is the old gray tanner who welcomed me, accepted me, fed me, and *warned* me of "madness," madness such as this...

Though we were complete strangers, I felt as though I was family under his roof. But I know full well that his love flowed not from a bond of blood or an austere devotion to Eusebian morays, but from a fount of faith in the god he served. It is because of this faith and a connection with me, an obstinate runaway who cared for no one but herself, that he is facing death as a cultist's sacrifice.

And Gennadius is not alone. Hesitantly, my eyes move past him to make out the imposing, unmistakable silhouette of Titus. And beside him, the long, raven-dark hair of Aspasia, an orange calendula flower tucked behind her ear.

I shut my eyes, hoping somehow that this is just another nightmare and that when I awake, I will be safe inside the Indigo Chamber with Anatolius and the others, or on the banks of the stream outside Eirene whistling with the birds and watching the Centaur steal the strawberries from the trees.

But not even Phobetor, the ghoulish god of the Alpha's land of dreams could envisage a phantasm as frightening as this. I know that written in the darkness and the blood, the smoke and the fire are living, indelible, unavoidable lines of prophecy. I know that I am standing in the epicenter of an imminent fulfillment of prophecy that has not yet reached its apogee.

"Your holy city has become a blaze, your altar a den of snakes,
Your holy house, once filled with praise, now in breathless silence quakes.
Your Courts of worship flow with fire, your children do not sing,
No trumpet sounds, nor flute, nor lyre...all is hushed by suffering."

Opening my eyes, I ask Duna to show me my next step, and for the strength to carry it out. If I am to use the doma, it will be because he commanded it. If I am to suffer, it will be because he has a purpose for it.

"Iris," says Tycho, placing a strong hand on my shoulder. "Iris, I will go. Follow me down the stairs and then get out of here as fast as you can. Do you understand?"

I shake my head. "No, Tycho. He wants us both."

Before Tycho can object, I jump up onto my feet and wildly wave my arms over my head.

"I'm up here, Diokles! Don't hurt them, I'm coming!" I shout at the top of my lungs, my blood thawing as a surge of boldness I've never felt rushes through me.

I feel Tycho press his lips to my fingers, and a moment later, he's standing beside me.

⁘

True to his word, Diokles orders the tormenters to return to their stations the instant Tycho and I show ourselves inside the Court. Exhausted from their strenuous efforts, the men hobble down the altar ramp – as if it was *they* who had been beaten – and fade into the restive crowd of horses and soldiers; its murmuring, snorts, and clinking armor imply its eagerness to watch our fate unfold. Only two guards stay behind - the ones with the largest arms and the meanest eyes.

With two quick twitches of his hand Diokles summons us onto the altar. I immediately go to Aspasia who is struggling to stand erect, but yet her placid smile appears unforced. She reaches out her hand to me and tries to speak, but Diokles grabs her hair and yanks her back.

"This is *not* a family reunion, you carcass-reeking crone!" he yells. "Keep your hands to yourself, or I will have Ariston cut them off!" The guard nearest Aspasia unsheathes his dagger and spins it in his hand with a barbarous scowl.

"Keep your eye on her," Diokles orders him. "On all of them!" He then points a finger at Captain Lycus who is seated on horseback below him; he signals to him with a single nod of his head. The captain pounds his chest, kicks his horse's flanks, and trots off through the rubble of the remaining western wall.

Where is he off to? I wonder. But I'm afraid I know exactly where...

"You said you would let them go," I say.

"Did I?" answers Diokles, tilting his chin to the sky. "I believe I said I would let them *live* and *not* go. You do see the difference...don't you? Or did I misjudge your intelligence?"

Diokles smiles tauntingly as he watches my fingers suddenly stiffen with what feels like a jolt of electricity. I hear Tycho exhale a puff of anger from his nostrils. He steps forward, closing the distance between himself and Diokles so none of the soldiers can hear:

"Let's settle this like civilized people, Diokles. There is no need to further defile Duna's Temple. Surely we can agree on that."

"Duna's Temple?" Diokles spreads his arms and spins around as he shouts, "Duna's Temple has fallen before your eyes, old friend! The time has come for the golden race to arise, and for the glorious comingling of gods and men. The throne of your jealous Duna has been usurped!"

Diokles drops his arms like clapping wings as a bird-shaped shadow falls over his face.

A bloodcurdling shriek sends a tremor of fear across the Court. The shadow circles us, spiraling down toward us with every revolution; its wings beat faster and faster, louder and louder, creating a cold, cutting wind.

Tycho looks up at the destroyer before I do, then draws me into his side and whispers, "Don't worry. We are more than conquerors. Our king has not forsaken us."

I take a breath.

The battering rams roll forward.

I let the breath out.

The last three towers fall.

I say a prayer.

The Gryphon lands before us.

I stare into her eyes, breathing steadily, praying ceaselessly.

"Iris, I believe you have met my most loyal assassin, your aunt Corinna," Diokles says softly, smiling as he strokes the creature's charcoal wing, a wing as long as he is tall. "And I believe you and Tycho were both aware of your fate should you choose to betray me."

Diokles turns to his men. "All of Ēlektōr knew the conditions of our deal! I was merciful. I gave Tycho another chance. I allowed you, a good-for-nothing orphan to publicly challenge my authority. And how did you repay me?! You snuck off after the man who pitied you, the hapless slave girl. You were soft. You are both so disgustingly *soft!*" Diokles removes his knife and throws it into the silver cup fifteen feet away, sending the priest's pure libation spilling over the altar's edge to be choked by blood and ash.

Corinna's yellow eyes glow. She throws back her head and cackles, filling the air around us with a thick, sulfurous smell.

"I only muzzle her when she isn't sure whom to kill," Diokles says. "But there was no need tonight. Remember, Tycho. Remember, Iris. This was your choice. I had marvelous plans for you. That doma of yours had been chosen by Apollo to...single-handedly, shall I say, decimate the entire Temple. And every Guardian, your master Acheron, one by one... You would have been greater than Corinna."

I hear Titus yelling, Aspasia crying, but they are silenced by the sentries within seconds. Diokles turns to the Gryphon, her wings unfurled and talons scraping across the dry stone floor. He parts his lips. She parts her beak.

"Attack!"

I shut my eyes and stretch my arms out wide, fiery darts blazing through me, coating my veins with the explosive resin. The hot air stings my throat as I take a deep breath in and let out a hasty prayer for accuracy, followed by a ringing shriek of pain, the fire now blistering beneath my skin. I lift my right hand, then my left,

And then...a heavy thud upon the altar. A shrill, dolorous wail. A few shuffling footsteps left and right.

"Who has done this?! Lycus!!!"

"Iris!" whispers Tycho. "The Gryphon has been killed!"

I open my eyes and turn to see the beast sprawled on the altar, at least twenty arrows sunk into her flesh. I drop my arms and watch smoke fly from my fingertips like ghosts escaping the pit of Hades, and exhausted, I fall against Tycho's chest.

"Let them go!" A girl's voice calls out among the squadron. "Reveal yourselves!"

Alexa, don't do this!

But it's too late. All eyes turn to the Naos, the holiest place of the Temple accessed by the high priest just once a year, and probably the last structure to remain standing until it can be plundered of its silver and gold and sacred vessels. On its roof, an archer arises. He turns and lifts his arms to the unseen psiloi behind him. They all stand and direct their attention to the voice calling out from the crowd:

"Surprised, brother?"

I watch in disbelief as waves of yellow hair tumble out of a Soukinoi helmet, its rider sitting calmly atop a gray, red-speckled mare. She drops her helmet to the ground and awaits Diokles's response.

"Yes, Alexa, I admit I wasn't expecting my own sister to try her hand at ambush. Especially not against me. But I shouldn't be, should I. I taught you everything you know about catching our enemies off guard...winning at their own game. Surprise nearly always proves a flawless strategy." Diokles steps to the edge of the altar and kneels down so his eyes are level with hers. "Unfortunately for you, dear sister, you have also learned much about treachery. I wish Apollo would have warned me of this. But then, perhaps he is testing me. We *all* must make sacrifices."

"That's just it, Diokles," Alexa says confidently, urging her horse forward through the motionless rows of soldiers, all watching her approach as though she were the archer-goddess Artemis, or the devious, war-loving Athena striding into battle. "Your loyalty to Apollo has driven you mad. You've forgotten who you are. You've turned your back on Duna, and your own people!"

"Silence!" Diokles shouts, his voice hissing and roaring all at once. "I will waste no more time trying to persuade you of what is coming – what *must* come! It seems your consciousness resists the age of transcendence. All who welcome it shall live on and evolve as gods, like Apollo and the lesser ruler, Duna. But the likes of *you*, well..."

Diokles raises his right hand as I've seen him do many times before pronouncing a judgment. He looks to the big guard, Ariston. "Bring her to me."

Diokles turns back to the Naos and addresses the psiloi, already drawing their bows, marking their target. He then points a finger at Aspasia, Gennadius, and Titus; three guards put knives to their throats.

"Psiloi, I don't know what my sister, the deluded princess, has promised you in return for your mercenary services today, but I can assure you that a generous portion of what lies in the Naos, just beneath your feet will be yours. All you must do now is toss those toys aside and come down from there. And stop this foolishness."

He waits a moment, and then another, but not a single soldier drops his weapon. All eyes watch as the captain in front strings his bow, wraps it in cloth, then carefully lowers it to his side. When he lifts it again, the arrow's tip is a ball of fire. The archers behind him follow, and soon the rooftop glitters with defiance.

"Ah...I see," says Diokles, his eyes narrowing, his jaws clenching. "This is a matter of *morality* to you all. You simply cannot break away from the myopic teachings of the old religion and the Oracles' pompous prophecies."

Ariston escorts Alexa up the ramp, but Diokles's patience is wearing thin. "Sword!" Diokles yells, advancing across the ramp to intercept them. A solider places his sword in Diokles's hand as he marches past. "All of you thought I would have pity on my own flesh and blood! I confess... I do," he utters. "I have pity on her indiscretion."

"I can't stay here, Tycho," I whisper. "Let me..."

As I speak the words, I tear myself from Tycho's arms and rip my dagger from my girdle. I race toward Diokles, arms pumping afresh with the doma's fire, heart pounding with the will to reach him before he reaches her, his own sister, merely a replaceable recruit in his eyes. But in mine, she is Jasper, the courageous martyr. Niobe the strong-willed slave. Corinna the rootless, defenseless Asher.

I cannot let her die.

CHAPTER TWENTY-EIGHT
VIOLET

Diokles doesn't hear me coming. *How does he not hear me coming?* It doesn't matter. I stay directly behind him, moving swiftly in a soundless blur.

I slow my pace when I see Ariston fall down dead, a flaming arrow between his shoulder blades.

"Iris!" Tycho yells.

I spin around to see Aspasia's guard charging me, sword in hand. Tycho slams himself into the guard's side, knocking the sword from his grip. The guard stumbles just enough for Tycho to push him again, this time face up onto the ground beside the Gryphon's body, which alarmingly now looks no larger than an eagle's.

Before the guard can right himself, Tycho pulls an arrow from the bloody mess of feathers and drives it into the man's throat. The guard's muscles relax;

his eyes roll back into his skull as his head falls with a terrible, gurgling moan. The Gryphon beside him seems to wither, her feathers shedding and falling away from peach-colored bones, bones that I soon see are not bones at all, but pristine skin, the skin of my aunt. Her long hair is auburn like mine, and out of her delicate shoulder blades flutter two wings, as grand as an eagle's and as violet as the Moonbow's last arch; a flurry of western wind moves them to appear breathtakingly celestial one last time, as they were always intended to be.

Tycho returns his attention to me; I watch his eyes widen with terror.

"Behind you!" he yells.

I turn and see Diokles wielding his sword, coming straight for me.

"And where do you think you're going, *sister*?" he fumes, the dark onyx spheres once again swallowing the cerulean color of his eyes. "After all I did for you. You were so close to avenging your brother. Isn't that what you wanted? How you have *failed*..."

I hold my tongue and my dagger steady.

Duna, fight for me. Defend me. My life is in your hands, not mine.

"Duna had a far greater reason to keep me alive than avenging Jasper." The words slide past my lips, a revelation too thrilling to contain. "I have failed to become what I wanted to be. And through Duna, that is my greatest victory."

Diokles's upper lip curls into a snarl. He growls, then bares his teeth, transporting my mind back to the hills around Enochos where I stared into the eyes of the gray wolf, my first kill. On that day, I had pretended the wild animal was Acheron. I'd made the first move, thrust my dagger through its heart, and began to imagine how satisfying the sight of Acheron's spilled blood would be.

Now, as I stand face to face with a second wolf, this one much more cunning and fierce than the first, I am overcome only by the desire to honorably defend, not vengefully attack. The spirit of "Hunter" has flown away from me;

the inner voice has been muted, just as Tycho said it would be. But now another hunter approaches...

"I'll make this fair," Diokles growls as he casts his sword aside. Then he charges me with his dagger raised. The darkness in his eyes now glows red, and I wonder if Apollo is within him now. His knife comes down.

Duna, I pray.

I dodge the blow and shuffle backwards, tossing my knife to the ground and letting the fire surface and seethe as hot as it will. I watch Diokles's pupils dilate at the sight of my flaming right hand; they are simultaneously attentive to it, and distracted by it...

I rush at Diokles and strike his wrist as hard as I can; his dagger falls and I kick it toward Tycho behind me.

"Kill him, Iris!" Tycho shouts.

I wrap my scorching hands around Diokles's throat and stare into his eyes, watching the enkindled blackness subside. The crystalline color floods his irises again.

"I don't want to kill you," I whisper to him.

"I don't want to die, sister," he replies, his chin quivering as his blue eyes hopelessly search the skies. "I'm – I'm sorry..."

I start to lower my hands, but as I do, I notice a faint smile dance across Diokles's lips, a flash of red in his eyes. As he raises his arm, I close my eyes and hold my breath as razor-sharp blades of fire pierce through my fingertips and plunge into his neck. I pull them out again to the cheers of the rooftop psiloi.

"I'm sorry," I say, my voice quavering through the ovation of voices and clapping hands. Diokles looks at me with roaming, vacuous eyes, smoke billowing from two black, bloody holes in his neck, as though he'd been bitten by a viper, or perhaps Python himself.

"You've accomplished nothing," Diokles rasps. "None of you have!" He grimaces and fights the fall to one knee. "The reign of Apollo *is* coming. And he will crush you all and laugh at death; it cannot touch him."

"There's still time, Diokles. Duna is patient with us." I whisper the words faintly, as if speaking any louder will make them vanish before reaching his ears.

He tilts his head and smiles curiously as his eyes begin to flutter and he collapses onto his heels. "What do you mean?" he says, straining to project every searing word.

"You can have eternal life. Just believe, Diokles. Ask Phos to save you. "

"Never!" he shouts, his outrage overwhelming his pain. Then his outrage gives way to death... "It...isn't...over... Do...you...hear...me..." He spews his last words, his own haunting knell, with wide, bloodshot eyes that churn both with terror and imprecation, and I know he means to threaten me, to threaten all of us.

"What do you mean?" I say, pressing my hands against his face, trying in vain to keep him alive one minute more. His eyes roll back into his head before he can take another breath.

"Brother!" I hear Alexa cry out. She runs to him, lying on his back with the implacable mask of anger still clinging to his face. "Brother, what happened to you..." She folds herself over his chest; her sobs fill the Court as Diokles's cavalry slowly abandons the altar and drifts away like a fleet of ships breaking up in a storm.

Tycho wraps his hand around mine, then lifts his eyes to the Naos where the archers are waiting, wondering like me, *What happens now?*

But Tycho doesn't have an answer or a command to give them. His lips part, but only a pensive sigh escapes them.

After a few moments, the psiloi leader aims an arrow at the guard standing nearest to Titus. He backs away without contest, and he and the guard beside Gennadius descend the ramp and follow the silhouettes of soldiers into the upset sea.

Aspasia reaches out her arms to me and I run to meet her. My eyes fill with tears at the sight of her bruised face and torn-apart flesh.

"Aspasia! I should never have left you. I'm so sorry!" I cry, holding her hands to my face as my warm tears wash over them.

"Shhhh, child," she smiles. "Duna is a wonderful craftsman. He works all things together for the good of those who love him. Broken fragments, broken hearts...all can be mended and made beautiful by his hands."

"Even when I didn't love him, he was pursuing me, Aspasia. I felt him. I tried evading him as best I could..."

"It is the greatest love, Iris. That is all. The greatest love." She kisses my forehead, and the kindness of it settles into my spirit; I feel the weightlessness of grace ridding me of my burden, carrying it into oblivion.

Titus and Gennadius join and pull us close, and together we huddle in reverent silence until Alexa approaches, now an orphan just like me.

"I prayed," she says quietly.

Titus and I exchange glances.

"What do you mean?" I ask.

"The day you saved Tycho at the bathhouse," she explains. "You seemed so brave, and my brother seemed so cruel. The only thing I knew to do was what I'd been taught a long time ago: *pray for wisdom.* The Oracles said wisdom is better than strength."

Gennadius smiles. "That's right. You had very wise parents for teaching you that," he says.

"I would like to find them. I followed Diokles to the desert." She looks over her shoulder at her dead brother and chokes back tears. "He told me I would be a princess for the rest of my life and would never have to take orders from an Alpha again. He told me a lot of things... I'm sorry about your aunt, Iris. I didn't know. I promise I didn't know," she says pleadingly, her voice shaking as she looks back at Corinna's body, now draped with a blanket.

"I believe you," I say. "He was deceiving all of us."

"We will pray that you find your parents," Aspasia says, touching Alexa's hand. "And we'll help. I promise."

"I found someone hiding at the bathing place."

I turn to see Tycho, and behind him the Centaur, soaking wet and chewing on a piece of wood.

"I thought I saw something suspicious from the roof earlier," adds Tycho. "A crate moving through the water and a black tail floating behind it."

"And what were you doing there while we were here fighting to survive?" I ask.

"I thought it best to keep myself scarce when I saw the Guardians running out of the city like shrews out from under a log when the battering rams started rolling in. Besides, who else is going to carry the old tanners back to Limén where the young rascal stole my sword?" He winks at Alexa. She jumps up and runs to him, then swings herself onto his back and wraps her arms around his shoulders.

"I missed you, Centaur," she says.

"Let's get the general and the tanners to a doctor," Tycho says. "The journey to Limén can wait another day or two."

"Iris," Alexa says, beckoning me with three bends of her forefinger. I go to her, and she leans in, placing a protective hand to my ear so no one can hear her ask, "What about Acheron? If he escaped with the other Guardians, he can't be far from here."

Without a moment's hesitation, I whisper my response, "I have been forgiven, having done nothing to earn it. And so is he. I think I will let Duna be his judge."

Alexa smiles broadly and hugs my neck. "It's a new beginning for us, isn't it?" she asks.

"Absolutely, sister," I say, helping her off the Centaur. "Our journey has just begun. And only Duna knows the way."

"And how to put that doma to use!" blurts the Centaur.

"Have you become a believer now, Centaur?" Titus asks.

The Centaur snorts a laugh. "I may need to witness just one more *trick.*"

"Don't tempt me, Centaur. I might just send a fireball into your skull to knock some faith into you," I reply with a wink.

"I think Duna has long ago forgotten about me," the Centaur says, glancing sideways at the stars, chin tucked and eyes shifting as if he feels unworthy to look upon them.

"Duna forgets about no one," Aspasia says, her fingers finishing a braid in Alexa's hair. Her head bobbing and brow softening, Alexa looks like a child again. I pray Duna will expel the nightmare of Ēlektōr far from her memory. No more swords and daggers. No more manhunts or sparring with Centaurs, unless of course it's with our Centaur...

"You know, Tycho," the Centaur begins, his eyes dropping to the serpent tattooed on Tycho's arm. He hesitates, then looks up at Tycho and searches his face like one who is examining an estranged friend to make sure he is who he claims to be. "It was you, in all your evil, who made me believe that Python truly did exist. What – or *who* – else could compel a man to do such unspeakable things? And now," the Centaur sighs, shaking his head in wonder of his forthcoming statement, "the fact that you stand in the presence of the kindest people I've ever known convinces me that I would be a fool not to have faith in a god of goodness. I suppose, Tycho, my fellow Pythonian, your faith has been like a doma to me – a true gift."

Tycho takes the Centaur's arm and embraces him, saying as much with that single gesture as he could with a thousand words.

"I think there might be hope for you after all, half-breed!" Alexa quips, apparently having discovered a second wind.

Titus helps Gennadius and Aspasia onto the Centaur's back, and Alexa follows the four of them down the ramp and onto the street as a soft shower of rain falls from heaven. I leave Tycho to look after Anatolius's and Corinna's bodies and make my way to the bathing place.

Sitting on the pool's edge I look up at the alabaster moon, a fearless lily blossoming from violet soil. Feeling its presence, I turn to see the Moonbow suspended above the Naos, each arch more vibrant than ever, each one glorifying its maker with its own unparalleled beauty. I think of the colors and the ways in which they called to me...

Red, the highest band, color of blood and vice;
I have learned to see within you redemption, sacrifice.
Orange, like the healing flower, and the burning desert sun;
Both have power, both hold brilliance, but none compares to the Promised One.
Yellow for the amber scrolls, prophesying salvation amid our strife;
Your shimmer is a just shadow in the light of eternal life.
Green for the stone I carry, a symbol of forgiveness, growth, and mirth;
But nothing can bring as much happiness as a dying soul's rebirth.
Blue, the color of Carya's sword that cut us free from prison;
But the greatest freedom I have felt flows from faith that Phos is risen.
Indigo, hue of an opaque void, the barrier between Petros and glory;
Its power has been stripped away by the Finisher of our story.
Now violet: triumphant, royal, reflecting clouds in this bathing place;
I will emerge boldly from these waters, an orphan found and saved by grace.

Diokles said it wasn't over, and as much as I would like to think he was rambling delusions and lies, I believe him. Dismantling Ēlektōr and killing its leader won't hinder Python's plan for this realm; there is far too much darkness pervading Petros than can be overthrown by any army, no matter how many domas it may have fighting on its side.

I will write this story as Asher wrote his, and will leave it for generations to come, so that they may learn and be reminded that evil is not weakened, let alone exterminated, by more evil. It must be conquered with good, and hope must never be lost.

The End.

Glossary

Acheron: Iris's master and man responsible for her brother's death; he is named after Acheron, the river of pain, which in Greek mythology was a stream and swampy lake of the underworld and its god[1]

Alexa: Diokles's younger sister; he name is the feminine form of the Greek word *alexo*, meaning "to defend, help" In *Moonbow*, Alexa's name foreshadows her role in Iris's story.

Alpha: polytheistic and/or agnostic people who rule Petros; Alpha is the first letter of the Greek alphabet from which the Alphas, the prominent ruling class of Petros, receive their name

Anatolius: the high priest of Eirene who name is derived from the Greek for "sunrise"

Asher: ancient ancestor of Iris; his name means "fortunate" and "blessed" in Hebrew

Aspasia: Gennadius the tanner's wife; her name is Greek for "welcome," "embrace"

Carya: an angelic messenger who appears to Iris; her name is inspired by the pre-classical mythology goddess of the walnut tree. In *Moonbow*, Iris notes that Carya is heard laughing from the treetops of a walnut orchard.

Corinna: Iris's aunt, also an Asher; her name means "maiden" in Greek

Diokles: leader of the Soukinoi; his name means "glory of Zeus" in Greek

---

[1]   http://www.theoi.com/Khthonios/PotamosAkheron.html (accessed October 22, 2014)

Duna: sole god of the Eusebians; his name is from the Greek word *dunamis,* which means power residing in a thing by virtue of its nature[2]

Eirene: Eusebian city; Greek for "peace"

Ēlektōr: Soukinoi desert fortress; Greek for "the beaming sun;" also related to *elektron,* meaning "amber"

Éleos: desert oasis where a group of peaceful priests dwell; its name comes from Greek word for "mercy"

Enochos: execution site; Greek for "involved in, liable"

Eusebian: monotheistic people group of Petros; from the Greek word *eusebia,* meaning "pious," "reverent," and "godliness"

Gennadius: tanner who welcomes Iris into his home to work; his name comes from the Greek for "noble" and "generous"

Ireneus: priest targeted by the Soukinoi; his name comes from the Greek for "peaceful"

Iris: main character of the story; her name comes from the Greek for "rainbow"; In Greek mythology, Iris was the goddess of the rainbow.

Jasper: Iris's deceased brother; his name means "jewel" or "gem" in Hebrew

Limén: Eusebian town; Greek for "a harbor" or "a haven"

Lycus: leader of Diokles's; his name comes from the Greek for "wolf"

Lysander: Soukinoi outlaw leader; his name means "the release of a man" in Greek

Niobe: a slave of Acheron's; her names is Greek for "fern"

Okeanos: stream where Iris first encounters the Soukinoi; its name is shared with the name of the river, or body of water, thought by the ancient Greeks to surround the Earth. In Greek mythology, Okeanos was the Titan who personified this body of water.[3]

---

2   http://www.biblestudytools.com/lexicons/greek/nas/dunamis.html (accessed October 22, 2014)

3   http://www.behindthename.com/name/okeanos (accessed October 22, 2014)

Petros: the world of the story; its name comes from the Greek for a small rock or pebble

Phos: Duna's son; his name comes from the Greek for "a source of light" and "radiance"

Psiloi: In Ancient Greek warfare, the psiloi were unarmored or lightly armored infantry trained as skirmishers.

Python: evil entity that rules Petros from beneath the Great Sea

Soukinoi: the Eusebian army of rebels; their names is derived from the Greek word *soukinos,* meaning "made of amber"

Titus: the Soukinoi general, named after the mythological Greek Titans who were primeval deities and giants of incredible strength

Tycho: former Soukinoi; his name comes from the Greek for "hitting the mark"

AUTHOR'S NOTE

Thank you for joining me in my first fantasy adventure. I hope you enjoyed reading as much as I did writing! If you loved the book and have a moment to spare, I would really appreciate a short review. Your help in spreading the word is gratefully received.

www.dianaandersontyler.com
Facebook.com/dianafit4faith
Twitter @dandersontyler
Pinterest @dandersontyler